THE GRAVE ROBBERS' CHRONICLES

VOL 6

Graveyard of a Queen

BY XU LEI
TRANSLATED BY
KATHY MOK

The Grave Robbers' Chronicles: Volume 6
Graveyard of a Queen
By Xu Lei
Translated by Kathy Mok

Edited by Janet Brown and Michelle Wong
Illustrated by Vladimir Verano

ThingsAsian Press
San Francisco, California USA
www.thingsasianpress.com
Printed in China

ISBN-13: 978-1-934159-36-1
ISBN-10: 1-934159-36-0

TABLE OF CONTENTS

CHAPTER ONE

CHASING WEN-JIN

How could Qilin tell that this ghostly figure was Wen-Jin? I couldn't decide if it was male or female myself—its face was completely covered with mud. But still we followed him as he raced toward the water. Swamp weeds caught at our feet and plunged us all into the dark, murky pool. Soon the water was deep enough to cover our heads and we began to swim.

Qilin caught up with his quarry and we came close enough to see the person we'd been chasing—she was a woman. Qilin rushed to her side but when he could almost touch her, she dove deep into the water, heading toward the darkness. As she disappeared, so did Qilin, swimming in her wake.

Panzi stopped me before I could follow them. "Don't bother—we'll never find her in that swamp. I don't think even Qilin will be successful."

"What the hell? Why did she run? Didn't she tell us to meet her here?" Fats asked.

"Who knows?" Panzi replied. "And who knows if that was really Wen-Jin."

"What do we do now?" Fats asked. "Qilin is out there in the darkness without even a flashlight. Should we follow him and help him if he needs it?"

Qilin needing *our* help, I snorted silently as Panzi said, "Probably not. That guy isn't like us—he knows what he's doing. If we went after him, he'd probably end up having to rescue us."

For the first time, I wasn't really certain that Qilin *did* know what he was doing. Somehow I felt he'd changed since we came to the swamp but I couldn't put my finger on that difference.

We waited for a while but Qilin didn't return. "Let's not stay here in the water," Fats begged. "Snakes will find us soon and I'm not ready to meet any more of them just yet."

Panzi and I followed him out of the pool and back to the swamp where our fire still flared brightly. We sat near its comfort, and my mind fell into a wild whirl of worries and fears. I knew that without Qilin, we were in bad shape. We had just begun our journey into the swamp and already Ning was dead, snakes had encircled us while we slept, there was a person out there who might or might not be a threat to us, and who knew what would be next? With Qilin behaving more strangely than usual, I was starting to feel as though this ought to be the end of our trail.

Panzi threw more wood on the fire, and the flames shot skyward. I picked up one of our strongest flashlights and turned it toward Ning's sleeping bag; it was oddly flat.

"This is insane," I yelled. "Ning—her body is gone!"

Panzi and Fats rushed over and kicked at the sleeping bag; there was nothing in it and it was surrounded by the muddy, slithering trail of reptiles. There were no other tracks nearby, and a quick search of the area yielded no sight of Ning's body nor any clues to tell us what might have carried it off.

"Even if the snakes returned, they couldn't have taken away anything as heavy as a human corpse," Panzi grumbled.

"Nothing else was here," Fats pointed out. "And look at all of these tracks. With this many snakes, they could have hauled away an elephant, let alone a body as small as Ning's."

"Why would they want it?" Panzi asked. "Even carnivorous reptiles won't eat dead flesh—and Ning wasn't even a fresh kill."

"Go ask the goddamned snakes." Fats paused and then continued, "It's so typical of this woman that even when she's dead, she's still a pain in the ass."

"We were only gone for a little while," I interrupted. "Whatever took the body can't have gone very far. Let's go look for it."

"What the hell are you talking about? There are hundreds of snakes in this place—why give them more victims?" Panzi asked as he grabbed me by the arm. "Listen to me. Ning is dead; her body is only a lump of dead meat now. We can't take her out of here; she's already beginning to rot. This place is her burial ground, wherever in the swamp she may be. Leave her in peace."

"That's right. Dead is dead," Fats agreed. "Doesn't matter where you die. But if I die here, you guys better burn my body—don't let those snakes take me away. Who the hell knows what they do with dead bodies anyway?"

He studied the marks in the mud. "Scary little bastards. How many of them do you think it would take to move a body? Got to be at least a hundred. Think about it. If there are that many of them right here near us, then how many snakes are in this entire swamp? We ought to start moving, forget about waiting for Qilin."

"Actually I don't think we need to be worried, they didn't bite us when we were sleeping just now," Panzi said. "I came across a few snakes in Vietnam and I've been bitten two or three times, so I'm pretty familiar with snakes in general. It's not likely that they'll launch an attack on us. Ning's death was an accident. When she was bathing in the waterfall, maybe she startled the snake that killed her."

Fats and I both knew that Panzi was just trying to keep us from going into a panic. These weren't ordinary snakes; I was certain they were evil, and intelligent too. And I was beginning to worry about Qilin; we all were.

We sat up all night, waiting for him, unable to sleep. When the sky finally brightened we felt a bit better, but the morning brought no sign of Qilin.

"Face it," Fats observed, "the worst that might have happened is he died last night and now we're on our own. Let's have some breakfast and decide what to do next."

When we finished eating, Panzi went back to the edge of the ravine and gathered up some dead branches.

"What are you doing with those?" I asked.

"Your uncle should be near the entrance of this canyon by now," he told me. "I'm going to start a fire and send him a smoke signal so he'll know we're here."

When the fire began to blaze, he threw a capsule into the flames and a stream of thick, yellow smoke rose into the sky. "I kept a bunch of these after I left the military," he said proudly, "just three of these babies will produce a cloud of smoke that lasts for hours. The yellow smoke means there's danger ahead so be cautious."

He added another capsule as the first began to die down; the second had burned for an hour or so when Fats yelled, "Look! We've got a response!"

A cloud of red smoke billowed up in the distance, lazily reaching the sky. But it wasn't coming from outside of the canyon—it rose from the depths of this swamp—and it was deeper into it than we were.

CHAPTER TWO
SMOKE SIGNALS

"Holy shit," Panzi muttered. "What's going on? How did they get ahead of us?"

"Well, Big Pan. It looks like your Master Three is faster than you," Fats taunted.

"That's impossible. Could they have come in from a different corner of the canyon? But that wasn't our plan; they were supposed to wait for my signal. And this is just too damned fast."

"Could this signal have been launched by Qilin and not Master Three's team?" Fats suggested.

"It can't be him," Panzi said. "Master Three and I are the only ones with these smoke capsules."

"That's strange. It seems like something's gone wrong with the communication between you and your Master Three."

"What does this red smoke mean?" I asked, peering at it through my binoculars.

Panzi took the binoculars from me and looked at the smoke. "Oh hell," he said. "There's been an accident."

"Accident? What do you mean?"

"Different colored smoke means different things," Panzi explained. "Yellow means danger ahead—proceed with caution. Orange means stop moving until told otherwise. Red is the most rarely used—it means don't come any closer."

"Can we send up another signal asking what's going on?" I asked.

Panzi shook his head. "No. there's only one thing to do. I have to go by myself and see what the problem is. Your uncle could be in trouble—I need to find out."

"You can't leave us—Qilin hasn't returned and I'm not going to rely on Fats for advice and protection. Just wait until Qilin gets back and we'll all go together."

"I can't wait. Your uncle has a team of more than thirty men—they wouldn't send up a red smoke signal unless something terrible happened. Don't worry—I'm a jungle veteran; I won't have any problems, and Qilin will be back soon to help you guys."

Panzi began to gather his gear and when I looked at Fats to back up my argument, I saw he was packing too. "Stop glaring at me," he snapped. "Panzi's right, but we all have to go check on your uncle. And we need to replenish our supplies or we'll die in this damned swamp. Panzi can survive without us, but you and I could very well join Ning if we stay here."

"What about Qilin?" I asked. "He won't know where we went when he comes back. Why don't I stay here and wait for him and then you guys can come back to join us?"

"Are you that eager to die? The snakes would make short work of you if we left you here alone, my book-loving friend. We'll leave a message for Qilin, telling him where we've gone and once we get to your uncle, we'll send up a smoke signal. But let me make this very clear—I don't think our poker-faced pal is coming back."

Fats made sense, although I hated to admit it. We divided up our supplies so we all carried the same weight, leaving Qilin's share behind. Carefully we wrapped his gear in a piece of waterproof cloth, put it in the shadow of the carved rock, and wrote a message to him on the wrapper in indelible ink. Near the pack, we built a small bonfire that we were sure would burn for three days. Even if Qilin returned after dark, he would see the flames and find his gear, and our message too.

"Your uncle's smoke signal won't last more than three hours so we have to keep moving toward it—no breaks," Panzi warned us. "We'll come back here after we find the others so don't take everything with us now."

We left our gas masks, our shovels, and other heavy items. Panzi insisted on taking some of my load. "I'm used to marching in the jungle. You aren't. We need you to keep up, so don't argue with me."

Just as we were ready to set off, Fats grabbed me. "The smoke—look at it." The signal was growing weaker, disappearing into the sky.

"We're not going to make it to your uncle if we lose that signal," Panzi said grimly. Quickly, compass in hand, he scrambled up the tallest tree he could find, orienting himself by using the distant cliffs as a marker. He returned with a clear direction in mind. "If we go toward this, we should hit the spot where the signal came from, but we have to pay attention. If we go off course by a matter of thirty feet, we'll miss the other team entirely and this jungle is so thick we'll never find them."

We set off, guided by the compass, moving as swiftly as we could. We were soon far into the swamp; the water became shallow and the tree roots were thickly intertwined beneath the pools we walked through. The daylight that trickled though the canopy overhead was scanty; the tree trunks were shrouded in moss. It felt as though we were moving through a moist, green cave. It was dead quiet, no birds, no wind, not even the hum of mosquitoes.

"Are we the only living things in this damned place?" Fats asked. "This swamp is getting on my nerves."

"You're not alone, Fats," I replied. "But let's not talk about it. We might attract some snakes—if there's anything alive here, they'd be the ones to flourish."

We walked in silence, not even exclaiming with surprise when ancient ruins jutted up from the depths of the pools ahead. They looked like towers and spires wrapped in a thick covering of vines, but we had no time to stop and examine them, nor were we able to see the parts of them that were underwater. They assured us that we were on the right track and were entering the Queen of the West's domain. At the tops of the spires were square holes, too small for a person to enter. Fats shone his flashlight into one as we passed, but we could see nothing inside it but darkness.

As we moved deeper into the swamp, the water level dropped even further, revealing many structures beneath the surface, all of them intertwined with tree roots. This had obviously been a large city, thriving and bustling many centuries ago. Now the eerie silence was even more disturbing as we made our way through the abandoned, underwater metropolis.

We passed a huge tree when Fats let out a yelp. There in front of us was a strange face, as big as an army tank. It had mottled green spots all over its countenance and looked exactly like the bird with a human face that had been carved into the cliff. But this was a statue, covered with moss and vines. Its body was underwater; only its massive head loomed above the surface.

We looked at each other, not daring to express our thoughts. If the carvings we found earlier were signposts that marked the beginning of the Queen of the West's empire, what did this mammoth counterpart represent? Was it a warning? What dangers lay beyond this statue?

CHAPTER THREE
THE MYSTERIOUS FACES

"What's that dark thing near the bottom of the statue?" Fats asked, peering into the water with his flashlight.

"It looks like a hole," I replied, "see how the water's flowing into it here?"

"Where do you suppose it's going?" Fats persisted. "Could there be a tunnel beneath this submerged city?"

"Maybe it's part of the ancient drainage system," I said.

"Where would it lead to? This is all lowland here, there's no lower point the water could flow into." Fats continued, "There are no rivers in the area that would carry this overflow to the sea, nor are there any big lakes either."

"This is a region where water is precious," Panzi interrupted. "There's probably a reservoir or two built to collect any surplus rainfall. Come on, stop wondering about useless matters while Master Three could be in danger."

Before we could pick up our pace, we were stopped by the snap of a tree branch. A rustling of leaves broke the eerie silence. We turned to look and as we did, all sound stopped. Panzi raised his rifle as Fats muttered, "What the hell? The head of that damned statue has turned completely around—it's looking at us."

It was impossible but true. The statue that faced us as we entered the middle of the swamp had turned on its neck and was staring in our direction.

"It even has a different expression on its face now," Fats whispered. "Could it be alive?"

Panzi gritted his teeth. "Only one way to find out." He fired his rifle and a branch near the statue splintered, sending a cascade of leaves all over the stone face. There was no motion from the carved figure, and we all smiled.

"We must have gone on a different angle when we passed this thing so that its face is still visible. Nothing to worry about—keep walking," Panzi assured us.

"I'm not so sure you're right," Fats argued. "Here, let me have your rifle for a minute." He grabbed Panzi's gun and walked toward the statue. He had only covered half the distance when he stopped and took a step backward.

"What the hell's wrong? Get back here," Panzi yelled. To our shock, Fats obeyed him. As he raced back to us, he yelled, "Run! That thing is alive!"

We stared in horror at the giant face. Its eyes gleamed and its mouth was upturned in a hideous smile. Then its features began to slide in different directions as though the face harbored something that was ready to hatch right now.

We all raced into the swamp as fast as we could, too terrified to think or even breathe. When I found enough courage to glance back at the statue, I saw it was still in the same spot and I felt a stab of grateful relief that it hadn't moved after us.

Fats and Panzi were ahead of me and I called for them to come back. We all gasped for breath as we looked at the motionless statue.

"What the hell? Do you think that we set off some kind of trap that made that face move?" Fats asked.

"We didn't even touch it—how could we have triggered any trap? But it's absolutely true that the face moved all the way around on its neck, and the damned thing smiled too."

"And that's not all," Panzi said slowly, peering through his binoculars. "Now it's turned back around again."

"What?" I pulled the binoculars from him and looked— sure enough, the back of the statue was now facing us. Its grim, ferocious face had disappeared.

"Give me those," Fats yelled. "What kind of craziness is this?" He slipped and almost fell. As Panzi and I steadied him, we turned slightly. Behind us was another mammoth face, carved in stone, staring at us blankly, looking just like the one that had scared us so badly just a minute ago.

"Look! They're everywhere," Panzi shouted. Surrounding us were those enigmatic faces, looking right through us. As we stared back at them, overwhelmed by what we saw, each of the faces cracked like an egg and bits of them began to float into the air.

Now I know I've gone insane, I thought, but then I heard Panzi yell, "It's a cloud of moths! Somehow they made a pattern of human faces as they rested on the rocks and then they moved into flight when we disturbed them."

The sky was covered with little flecks of black, like tiny petals of dark flowers. Soon they flew off and disappeared, leaving us feeling foolish and very relieved.

"What's that white stuff over there where the moths were?" Fats asked, moving toward one of the rocks. "Oh

3. THE MYSTERIOUS FACES

shit," he continued, "it's skin sloughed off by snakes. And there's a hell of a lot of it."

We walked to where he stood and were horrified. There were hundreds of discarded skins heaped about us. How many snakes lived in this place? I didn't want to think about it.

"They're the same shape as the one that killed Ning," Fats announced. "Look, here's a whole skin with the head attached—it's as big around as my thigh."

"This is where they come to shed their skins, that's for sure," Panzi said. "And the skin you found was just recently sloughed off. The snakes obviously feel this is a safe place. If they find us here, they're certain to feel threatened and we'll all be dead meat in no time. It's time to get out of here right now, damn it."

We rushed on our way, keeping an eye out for reptiles and seeing none. Hoping they were nocturnal, I walked even faster, desperately wishing that my uncle had found a camp that was free of snakes. We ate as we walked, not daring to stop, passing waterfalls and caves, surrounded by an almost impenetrable jungle that we had to hack our way through.

"We've walked for at least five hours and there's still no sign of my uncle—have we gone too far?" I asked.

"Let me climb this tree and get my bearings," Panzi said. His voice floated down in a matter of seconds, "I can still see a trace of the smoke—we're almost there. Just a bit more walking—we can do it."

We kept going and as we advanced, I felt my vision begin to blur. Things in the distance looked fuzzy; even the trees looked indistinct. How could I be this tired? I wondered. Then I heard Fats say, "Holy shit. Where did this fog come from?"

I rubbed my eyes. He was right; the air was full of a gray mist that obscured everything. Suddenly the jungle became very cold and I felt as though something had wrapped around my body, squeezing my chest. Wheezing and shivering, we kept walking, even though we could barely see anything at all.

"Panzi, we're going to get lost in this fog. We need to stop," I said. "We can't see any farther than three feet ahead."

"You're right," he agreed, "but once it disperses then we have to keep going, even if it's after dark."

We collapsed on a dead tree that rested in the mud and made a flat, benchlike surface. Fats collected enough dried vines to make a small, smoky fire and we did our best to relax. I had almost dozed off when I heard Fats say to Panzi, "If we reach the site of the smoke signal and the team isn't there, what's your plan?"

"If Master Three is alive, I have to find him. If he's dead, then I have to recover his corpse. What's on your mind, Fats?"

"I came to make a fortune," Fats replied, "not to wipe your Master Three's ass. He didn't follow his own plan and he's screwed everything up. When Young Wu was awake, I didn't say anything because I didn't want to upset him. But now I'm going to put the ugly truth out in the open. If your Master Three isn't where you say he is, then I'll take my share of equipment, go it alone, and get down to business. I'm not going to follow you around on a goose chase in this fucking swamp."

"Take off on your own? We can barely survive in this place all together—not to mention those miles of desert that surround us. Even if you find some treasure and get it out of here without dying, how are you going to get across the Gobi Desert alone, you fool?"

Fats laughed. "Who do you think I am? I've got it all planned out. I'm just telling you in advance so you don't have to worry about me later."

Panzi shook his head and sighed. "Do what you want but

don't expect us to pull you out of whatever mess you fall into on your own—and don't think you'll be entitled to a share in whatever we find after you've gone, you stupid bastard."

"Sure, right. Why do you think Qilin disappeared? He knew the only way to get anything good was to ditch you people— and I'm just as smart as he is."

This made me laugh—I couldn't help it. Qilin would never have left us for money; I knew that for certain.

"What? The boy's awake? Go back to sleep and let us adults talk in peace," Fats taunted. He fell silent and this time I really did fall asleep.

CHAPTER FOUR
THE BRACELET

I woke up in pain, with every muscle in my body refusing to move. Fats sat nearby, staring at a tree. "Where's Panzi?" I asked.

Fats put his finger to his lips and silently pointed at the tree that absorbed his attention. Trying not groan, I hauled myself to my feet and walked to where he sat. Through a ribbon of moonlight that peeked through the mist, I thought I could see someone in the tree.

"Panzi?" I mouthed silently and Fats nodded, whispering, "He thought he saw something moving so he climbed up to get a better look."

Then we saw Panzi frantically waving for us to come up and join him. The damp and foggy air had made the tree trunk and branches slippery and treacherous so our ascent was slow. When we got to the spot where Panzi waited, the fog made everything below our perch look almost supernatural.

"Look over there," Panzi whispered. "There's a person up in that tree."

"How can you see anything in this misty darkness? Is it Qilin?" I asked.

"Doesn't look like him," Panzi hissed back. "Here. Take

the binoculars."

By now Fats's keen eyesight had adjusted to the dark. "There's really someone there," he agreed.

I focused the binoculars toward the spot Fats was pointing to and saw someone crouching in the branches near the top of the tree.

"Could it be the figure Qilin thought was Wen-Jin?' I asked.

"Could be," Panzi muttered. "It's why I told you to be quiet. If she hears us, she'll be on the run again. We have to figure out how to get to her. The mist is rising—we have to get to the bottom of her tree, grab her somehow before she can see us, and then keep looking for Master Three."

"Wait a minute," Fats interrupted. "There's something wrong here. Look at her wrist and you'll see what I mean."

I squinted through the binoculars and then almost dropped them. Through the lens, I could clearly see a bracelet made of coins—Ning's bracelet.

"Holy shit," I gasped. "Did the snakes move her body all this way and up that tree? How did they manage that?"

"Who the hell cares?" Fats replied. "It would have taken a whole colony of them to do that—that means we have to get out of here fast."

Panzi was silent. He had taken the binoculars from me and was staring through them as though they were glued to his face. His hands shook a little and his forehead gleamed with sweat.

"What's the matter?" I asked.

"Not a thing. Let's go now. Fats is right," he said.

We scrambled down hastily, grabbed our bags, and set off once again, Panzi turning his head to look back at the tree several times. Then he stopped, raised his hand, and muttered, "Quiet."

We all stopped, and as we stood we heard a weak voice, breaking the silence of the swamp. It sounded like a woman and it came from the tree that held Ning's body.

"God damn it," Fats whispered. "Has that little bitch decided to haunt us?"

"Shut up, Fats." But even as I said it, flickering shadows in the mist made his theory seem quite plausible.

"Maybe it's the person Qilin chased—we were all pretty sure she was a woman. But we shouldn't let this distract us from finding your uncle's group," Panzi warned us. "The problem is if we're going in the direction where the smoke came from, we have to walk past the tree where the voice is coming from." He pulled the bolt on his rifle into firing position.

Then he froze again. "Listen. I can hear what she's saying. Young Master Wu, she's calling your name."

"This damned swamp really is haunted," Fats whispered. "It has to be Ning—she's the only woman around who would know your name, Young Wu. She's probably lonesome and has chosen you to be her companion throughout eternity."

"Could she possibly be alive?" I wondered.

"You saw for yourself—her body was beginning to rot. Of course she's not alive."

"She's trying to lure us back to her side," Panzi said. "We need to find a detour—follow me and watch out for snakes."

The three of us turned to leave, ignoring the strange voice. The more I tried not to listen, the more the voice seemed to be living inside my head—but it didn't sound as though it was a person talking. The sound was crisp and made the same noise over and over; it sounded familiar and I stopped to listen. "It's Ning's portable radio. I'm sure of it. It must still be on her body and it's picked up a new transmission. We have to get it and listen."

"You're right," Panzi agreed while Fats argued, "Who would be calling her and how could the signal make it past the cliffs and through this swamp?"

"She's on a treetop. If the other person is at a high elevation, the signal could get through. Panzi, did my uncle bring a radio with him on this trip?"

"No, but there was a radio in our jeep. Maybe the driver saw the red smoke signal and maybe he's calling for reinforcements to rescue Master Three."

"We have to get that radio from Ning's corpse so we can talk to whoever is transmitting and find out how Uncle Three got ahead of us. Maybe we can get back to the vehicle and manage to reach my uncle without slogging through this snake farm."

"What are we waiting for? We need that radio," Fats yelled.

"Slow down," Panzi cautioned. "There may not be a ghost to worry about but there still are snakes. We need to build a fire to keep them away from us."

Fats began to gather kindling while Panzi looked grimmer than ever. "Panzi," I asked, "what did you see in that tree?"

"There's something wrong with that body," he began but Fats broke in.

"Did Ning have the face of a snake and was she staring

at us the whole time?"

"How the hell did you know that?"

Fats didn't reply, but pointed behind us. Panzi and I turned and saw a shadow sitting in the darkness, with radio noises emitting from its body.

"Is it really Ning?" Panzi whispered.

"Well, that sound is the same one that we heard a minute ago. We thought we were getting closer to it but instead it was following us. It's Ning's radio, that's for sure." My voice trembled as I spoke. Panzi's question echoed unanswered; none of us had gotten a good look at the figure in the darkness.

"That's not the only noise," Fats said. "Listen to those rustling sounds in the trees. My guess is that's the slithering motion of snakes that we're hearing, as well as that infernal radio. It seems to me as though they have us surrounded, my friends."

"It's time for fire. Duck down," Panzi ordered. He pulled out his camp stove and quickly opened its fuel tank, then pulled a tarp to cover the three of us and emptied the tank over our improvised tent.

"Grab this tarp and don't let go of it, even if your hands begin to burn," he told us. "When I say 'go' we'll start moving forward."

The rustling sounds were getting louder. Panzi pulled out his lighter and ignited the tarp. He darted back under it and yelled, "Run!"

Clutching the blazing tarp, we raced into the swamp as fast as we could go. When we had gone about a hundred feet, Panzi shouted, "Let go of it now." We released our portable bonfire and ran even faster. When we finally stopped, we heard nothing, not even the radio transmissions.

"Looks like we got away," Fats said, no longer whispering. "Panzi, that was an incredible scheme—do we have more tarps in case we need to do that again?"

"Tarps, yes," Panzi panted, "but only one more stove that has enough fuel. So hurry up—we're almost out of magic tricks and who knows where those snakes are now?"

We pushed on, ignoring our exhaustion, following Panzi's compass. I could hear Fats wheezing like a sick child, and then his voice boomed into the night. "I hear the snakes again. Did we go around in a circle? Are we back where we started from?"

He was right. The swamp was suddenly filled with rustles again, like ghostly whispers.

"We've never been here before," Panzi said. "They sent for reinforcements to surround us. We've been outmaneuvered. These aren't ordinary snakes—they're demons."

"What can we do?" I asked.

"Retreat," Panzi said.

"Just a minute," I argued. "Think this through. That first snake killed Ning in a second. These others have had a hundred opportunities to do away with us—why haven't they? Why are they delaying? Are they playing with us? It's clear that they don't plan to kill us—are they trying to frighten us? Warn us away?"

"This doesn't make sense," Panzi muttered. "If they don't plan to kill us, why did they kill Ning?"

"What was the basic difference between Ning and us?"

"You mean they killed her because she was a woman?"

Fats asked me in return.

"I think that's possible. And I think we need to figure out why that made her their prey and not us, rather than rushing into a situation that is even more dangerous. We need to outthink these creatures, not outrun them."

"How are we going to think like a reptile?" Fats sneered.

"We can analyze the behavior of humans, why not animals? Especially ones that seem to have a purpose—we ought to be able to figure out why the only woman in our group was killed and we're still breathing."

The three of us fell silent. Then Panzi took a deep breath and exploded into speech. "I think I know what's going on here. Have you ever heard of the kind of forest where you can't get out after you go in? It's easy to get lost in any forest but this particular kind is governed by some sort of supernatural law. They're characterized by strange, disorienting noises that make anyone who enters become confused and lost forever. People who live near them say these places have a will of their own."

"I don't know about that, Panzi. It seems more likely to me that the snakes are encircling us."

"It's much the same sort of thing," Panzi explained. "They're herding us into a direction we don't want to go in, as though we're cows, and that's confusing us. We don't dare to move toward the sounds, but we can't go back either; it's almost as though we're being enclosed by invisible walls. I know there's a type of wolf that hounds its prey to death like this. When the prey moves away from the sounds of the wolves, it's led to the edge of a cliff. Then it has no choice but to plunge to its death. If we take a detour, we'll fall into that same sort of trap.

"There's no turning back for us," he continued. "We're blocked ahead and behind, so we have to face them head on. If you're right, and they don't intend to kill us, we're not taking too big of a chance by doing this."

"We know our knives and the rifle aren't going to do us much good," Fats observed. "So let's use fire—we can each carry a torch and rush toward them. If we put them off guard with flames, maybe Panzi will have time to shoot and then reload his gun. Or so we have to hope."

"Remember," Panzi warned, "we don't know what we're facing. Yes, there are snakes, but who knows what that human shape really is. Our aim should be to get through the barrier ahead with no recklessness. We need to keep our heads clear."

We lit three torches and slowly walked toward the rustling sounds. As we drew closer, the sound of the radio became more and more distinct, but still I couldn't make out any words at all. It almost sounded as though it came from above our heads. We stopped moving and peered up into the nearest treetops but saw nothing.

Quietly and slowly, we resumed our advance, with the radio getting louder as we walked. Suddenly the sound stopped and the jungle became dead quiet. Then a voice came from a nearby tree. "Who's there?"

Panzi burst into a grin. "It's me—Big Pan. Are you part of Master Three's group? Which one are you?"

Quickly the tree fell silent again, and Panzi repeated, "Can you hear me? Who are you?"

He raised his torch and the voice called once more, "Who's there?" It sounded like a man who was in pain.

"I'm going up to find out who this is," Panzi said. "Here's my rifle; cover me while I climb, Fats."

As he rapidly scaled the tree, its leaves shook violently, but Panzi's pace didn't slacken. He disappeared from view and we waited for him to call down to us. There was no noise at all and the leaves went still. Minutes passed with no trace of Panzi. Fats looked at me questioningly and mouthed the word "Trap?"

As we stared up at the tree, something wet and cold dripped down our faces. When I touched it, my fingers felt sticky. "Hell," I whispered. "It's blood."

Fats opened fire, the treetop shook again, and under the light of my torch I saw the shadows of snakes writing on the tree trunk above us. Red flashes darted down the tree and cockscomb snakes—hundreds of them—covered the entire trunk like a river of blood. They hissed forward, striking at us.

"Fuck it! We've found a nest of the damned things," Fats screamed as he fired another volley at the deadly swarm. "Run!" he yelled, tugging at me.

I knew there was nothing we could do for Panzi. We raced back to where we had been, but the snakes were right behind us. We turned to face them and all of them raised up, poised to strike.

I still held my torch. Fats grabbed it from me and threw the rifle in my direction, shouting, "Reload." I missed the catch, the gun fell to the ground, and when I reached for it, a snake hurtled on top of the rifle.

"Damn you, you clumsy oaf," Fats shrieked. Charging toward the gun while brandishing the torch, he drove the snakes back, including the one on the rifle. He kicked the weapon toward me and this time I grabbed it. As I reloaded, I felt a dreadful coldness on my neck. Fats brought the torch so close to my head that my earlobe burned, and a snake dropped to the ground. He grabbed the rifle from me and fired, but the snakes still advanced, pushing us back against a tree trunk. Our torch was all that kept us from certain death and its flame was losing strength.

A hissing sound came from a tree nearby, then a shower of sparks, followed by an explosion. A fireball roared through the jungle, hitting the snakes near us before it exploded. "It's a signal flare," I shouted.

Another orb of fire whooshed from the darkness, landing

near our feet and igniting our clothing. We rolled in the mud to extinguish the flames.

We could smell the charred flesh of roasting snakes and when our eyes recovered from the blinding flash of the flares, we saw reptiles blazing at our feet. A tree rattled beside us and out came Panzi, one hand holding a flare gun and the other clutching his bloody shoulder. When he saw us, he fell to the ground. I rushed over to help him to his feet and as he stared up at me he gasped, "Run."

Before I could move or even think, a huge shadow emerged behind Panzi, grabbed him by the leg, and dragged him into the bushes. His screams cut through me like a knife.

4. THE BRACELET

CHAPTER FIVE

RESCUING PANZI

Fats jumped toward me, yelling, "Give me some bullets." I slapped a round of cartridges into his hand, which he jammed into the rifle. He raced into the bushes where Panzi had disappeared and I followed. We ran for a hundred feet or so before we found a tree shaking violently. "It's taking him up there," Fats wheezed. "And whatever has him is huge—look at that tree move."

We ran to the bottom of the tree and saw fresh claw marks on its trunk; as we looked, the treetop began to lean toward the one next to it. "It's going to jump over to that tree!" Fats yelled, aiming his rifle toward the mass of quivering leaves above us.

"Careful," I screamed. "Don't hit Panzi."

"He could be dead already," Fats replied. "It's a gamble I'm willing to take." He shot blindly into the treetop; the leaves continued to shake. He fired again, with no apparent results. The monster managed to leap to the next tree and then it disappeared.

"Look at this," Fats said, turning his flashlight toward the tree with the claw marks. Its trunk dripped with blood. He rushed toward the tree that the monster had leaped into; blood seeped down its trunk as well.

"I hit it!" he shouted. "We have a blood trail to follow—let's go!"

We had less than half a box of bullets left; Fats took five of them, putting three in his shirt pocket and two in his mouth. We followed the fresh blood into the jungle. It was no longer visible on tree trunks but the bushes glistened bright red. Was it from the monster or Panzi, I wondered. The trail became less bloody as we went farther along and I was afraid that Panzi might have bled to death.

Fats grunted and fell in his tracks; in front of his path was a blood-soaked backpack—it was Panzi's. He was back on his feet in an instant and clapped his hand over my mouth. Raising his flashlight high in his other hand, he jerked his chin toward an immense shadow, hanging down from a tree behind us. Before we could register what it was, it leaped toward us, coiling itself around Fats.

Fats rolled away from its grasp, and his flashlight revealed the shape of a giant python, covered in blood, with bullet holes on its body. It looked exactly like the largest of the two pythons that had attacked us before Ning died. Could it have been stalking us all this time?

It struck out again. Its jaws closed on Fats and it coiled around him again, pulling him into midair. Fats tossed the rifle to the ground and screamed as he careened like the propeller of a damaged airplane. I fired but missed, hitting the tree next to the one Fats was near. As I took aim again, I heard a faint voice from the tree I had hit. "Give me the gun." It was Panzi.

I looked up and saw his bloody arm reach toward me. I tossed him the rifle; he aimed and fired—but not at the python. With three well-placed shots, he hit the branch the python had climbed upon, snapping the wood to bits. Both the python and Fats plummeted to the ground.

The snake began to coil again but Fats had escaped its grip and rolled to my side. Immediately he began to vomit, his face scarlet and swollen. Is he poisoned or have his guts been crushed to fragments? I wondered.

Shaking him, I shouted, "Tell me if you're all right!"

"Damn," he choked out, "I'm dizzier than if I'd been on a roller coaster. Give me a minute—I'll be okay."

As he staggered to his feet, the python rushed over, grabbed him by the shoulder, and pulled him away. It hurled Fats against a tree trunk and he screamed as he hit the ground. The snake arched its head and opened its jaws, ready for a lethal strike, but before it launched itself at Fats, a tree branch landed on its head.

It looked up, saw Panzi, and changed direction, racing up the tree toward its new prey. As it approached, Panzi jammed his rifle into the python's jaws. Muffled explosions hit the air and rifle shots ripped the python's throat to shreds. It began to writhe in wild paroxysms of pain, throwing Panzi into the treetops and sending branches into the air. They rained about me like mammoth hailstones and I covered my head with both hands. When I dared to look up again, I saw the python, motionless, on the ground.

Dimly, through my terror and shock, I heard a voice moaning and realized it was Fats. He was almost unconscious; as I helped him to his feet, he babbled something incoherent and began to vomit again. I left him and went to find Panzi, who was sprawled on the ground twenty feet away. He was covered in blood, still clutching his rifle; as I approached him, he stared at me silently, spitting up large gobs of blood.

I took off his tattered shirt and almost vomited myself. His chest and belly were full of puncture wounds, but his battle-scarred skin was tough. The bites didn't go deep, I found, as I began to clean them with water from my canteen. He struggled as I worked, raised one arm, and jammed something into my hand. It was his compass.

"Find Master Three…Be careful…The python will…" He went into a convulsion, unable to speak.

I didn't know what he meant, but it didn't matter right now. He was having trouble breathing and continued to spit up mouthfuls of blood.

I found some antibiotics in his bag and forced a couple of capsules down his throat, hoping for the best. Fats staggered over, asking, "How is he?"

"I have no idea," I muttered. "But he saved our lives—we have to do what we can to save his."

I checked Panzi's pulse; it was stronger than I would have expected, judging from his labored breathing. I examined him thoroughly, looking for the wound that had caused him to lose so much blood, and found it on the back of his left thigh. It was quite deep but the blood had already clotted.

"We have to clean this and stitch it up somehow or he'll lose his leg to infection," I told Fats. "But we lost our first aid equipment—we need to find my uncle's group as fast as we can."

I took out Panzi's compass but neither Fats nor I knew how to read it. Shaking his head, Fats said, "Okay, let's wait for dawn. It can't take that much time to get to where your Uncle Three is. We're covered in blood and that's going to attract predators; it's safer to stay here for now. Besides, Panzi needs a break. He won't survive a long trek the way he is now."

It was true. Panzi had been almost superhuman but this injury made him useless and immobile. I covered him with all of our spare clothing to keep him warm and tried to make him comfortable. My own body was slow to the point of being robotic; all I wanted to do was collapse.

I sat down for a drink of water while Fats picked up Panzi's rifle. "Look at this thing. Panzi's brilliant. He blocked the barrel opening with a piece of his shirt so the gun would explode in the python's throat and break its spinal cord. Otherwise, it wouldn't have been easy to kill that bastard."

This was certainly true. When we were in the canyon earlier, every single one of Panzi's shots hit the python, and all of them together had almost blown its head off. It should have died then, but instead it lived to seek its revenge.

Fats said, "This damned snake had a brain. It seemed to remember Panzi from all those gunshots and it's been tracking us all along, waiting for the opportunity to attack."

I took the flashlight, stood up, and examined the python's body. It was huge, covered with golden-brown scales, each one the size of my palm. I cautiously walked to the side of its head; its tongue was still moving.

"Shit," I said. "This monster is still alive."

Grabbing his machete, Fats growled, "I'll fix that." He struck at the python's head but his blows left not even a mark on its scales. They were like armor, and there were two layers of them, with rough, thick skin under that.

Fats jammed his hand in one of the bullet wounds. "Be careful," I yelled. He yelped and brought his hand out; clinging to it was a tiny grass tick. I burned it off and then felt a stinging sensation on my leg. I touched the spot and found blood on my fingers.

"They're everywhere," Fats hissed, and the beam of his flashlight showed that our legs were covered with these insects. Ticks swarmed all over the bushes and tree trunks nearby.

These little insects were bloodsuckers and had no doubt been lured by the bleeding python. They were ravenous and quite happy to have found Fats and me. Fats set Panzi's ruined rifle on fire and we burned as many of our tormentors as we could. Then we picked up Panzi and took off, leaving the ticks to feast on the snake.

We carried Panzi to the edge of the swamp, where we washed him and ourselves thoroughly to get rid of the reek of blood. As dawn broke, I hoped with all of my strength that this would be our last night in this jungle.

"Which way should we go?" Fats asked me, and I shrugged. "Since neither of us can read the compass, I'll go up this tree and see what lies before us."

The morning air was cool and fresh; I stared from the vantage point of the treetop, expecting to see nothing more than a green roof of leaves. But instead, quite close by was a temple, towering and dilapidated, built from black stones. It was multileveled, with walls covered in bas-relief carvings.

I scrambled back to Fats, and carrying Panzi, we made our way out of the jungle and into the clearing where the temple stood. It looked a lot like Angkor Wat, with long, straight corridors and a multitude of stone towers. Even Fats was speechless for a minute, until he gasped, "Look—it's a miracle."

I thought that was a bit exaggerated until I followed his gaze. On the flat land near the temple were at least a dozen large tents.

CHAPTER SIX
REUNION

"It's your uncle's camp!" Fats shouted. "I know those tents."

A burst of excitement gave us new energy and we ran toward the camp. The area where the tents were placed was flat, wide, and filled with large pools, all fed by clear, flowing water that emerged from huge drains. The temple rose out of the largest pool, which was almost a lake, and I wondered how much of the structure was underwater.

As we approached the tents, Fats began to call out different names but nobody answered. The camp was weirdly silent and we stopped at its edge, realizing it had been abandoned.

"Too late," Fats muttered, and I fought back tears of disappointment and exhaustion. I wanted so much to collapse into my uncle's leadership; this damned swamp jungle was making me insane.

We lowered Panzi to the ground and walked into the campsite, our knives drawn. It was equipped beyond my wildest dreams with an electric generator and a kitchen stove.

A huge canopy seemed to serve as a kind of office, where documents were placed on a flat stone slab with smaller rocks serving as paperweights. There was a spot where toothbrushes had been left in a neat row, and a clothesline had been put near one of the pools. It was as though a little village had been set up here.

We peeked into every tent and found only the stink of sweat. There were no signs of violence anywhere, no bloodstains or broken items—but no people. It looked almost as if everyone had gone on a hike.

In the middle of the camp was the site of a huge bonfire. It was dead and traces of exhausted flares were nearby. This had to have been where the red smoke had come from, the signal that warned us to keep away. Why hadn't we paid attention?

Fats found a pack of cigarettes and lit one. He was too exhausted to manage more than a couple of puffs and when he handed it to me, I could do no better. But the nicotine gave us another surge of strength and we used it to carry Panzi into one of the largest tents. Inside it were two backpacks, a flashlight and a watch—even an MP3 player.

Fats went out to forage through the other tents and returned with a fully equipped first aid kit. At last we could clean Panzi's wounds properly, and Fats stitched up the gaping hole in his leg with the skill of a surgeon. "Should I make a needlepoint design in his skin?" he asked, and although I appreciated the joke, I was too tired to smile.

"Look at all the scars on this guy," Fats continued. "I once worked with an old soldier who was just like Panzi—after the war was over, he had to keep risking his life, almost like he felt guilty for surviving when so many others died. It was like everything he did was a suicide mission and when given a choice, he always took the dangerous route. No wonder your uncle always has Panzi on every expedition he makes—this man will take risks nobody else would dare to try."

We left Panzi and went outside. "There's something horrible about this place," Fats said, looking at the empty camp."We should get the hell out of here now while we still can. Let's gather up what we can use from these tents and take off now."

Slowly we rose to our feet and each took a step. Then we looked at each other with the same thought. Our bodies refused to go any farther. We were trapped here by our depleted muscles and spirits.

"Oh hell, it's probably not safe to return to the jungle right now anyway," Fats said with a shrug. "I'd rather die here in comfort listening to that MP3 player than shivering and wet in that damned swamp."

I shuddered as I realized that if we were to return to safety, we had to walk through the army of snakes again. And this time we'd be weighted down with Panzi—it meant a certain death sentence for us all.

Fats looked at me and shook me by the arm. "For once that brain of yours is going to do you no good at all. Let's see what food our missing comrades left for us."

We ate and then cleaned our own injuries, bathing in one of the pools. Grabbing clean clothes that hung on the clothesline, we threw away our own stinking, bloodstained garments. Revived by the tea Fats had made, I took the first watch as he slumped into sleep, a cigarette drooping from his lips. I pulled it from his mouth and puffed away, hoping that the nicotine and blazing sunlight would keep me awake.

I took shelter under the canopy where the documents were safeguarded and suddenly remembered Wen-Jin's notebook in my pack. Was it even useful now? She had first come to this place twenty years ago; two decades' worth of jungle had sprouted up since that time. It was true she wrote about "many snakes" but she failed to mention their deadly power—only their number. Had they become more aggressive over time or was Wen-Jin just not very bright?

Hoping there might be a clue as to how she had gotten out of this place so long ago, I flipped to the last page but my tired eyes refused to focus on the words. I was nearly asleep when I heard Panzi calling me. I jerked back to consciousness, but no voice emerged from the tent.

Am I hallucinating? I asked myself, but then I heard laughter from the middle of the campsite and an indistinct voice that sounded as though it might be complaining. Rushing toward the sounds, I found nobody and once again everything was terribly quiet.

Baffled, I went back to the canopy and lit another cigarette, feeling sure that I was losing my mind. Then I saw them—footprints in front of me and mud on the documents under the stones. Wen-Jin's notebook had been moved from the spot from where I had been reading it and there was mud on its cover. I followed the footprints; they led straight into Panzi's tent.

There was no time to awaken Fats. I picked up a large stone and approached the tent. A muddy handprint was visible on its nylon flap. I gulped hard, with my rock in attack position, and entered the tent. In front of Panzi squatted a man, covered in mud.

Shouting, I lunged toward the figure. He turned to face me. It was Qilin.

I could only recognize him by his eyes; the rest of him was

caked in mud, even his hair. He looked like a mummy; it was hard to believe he could have gotten that dirty after only two nights in the swamp. He stared at me and asked, "Do you have any food?"

I put down my rock and we walked out of the tent. He silently gulped down some food, his face as expressionless as a statue. Then he began to talk in one of the longest spates of words that I had ever heard from him.

"When I ran off to catch Wen-Jin, I chased her for six hours nonstop, but I lost her in the jungle—and then I found I was lost too, I had no gear with me—not even a flashlight or matches—so I could see nothing in the dark but I figured I couldn't have gotten too far from you guys. I sat and waited for daylight, not wanting to stumble farther away from you that night. Then when dawn came, I saw two different smoke signals, returned to where you had been, and found your message. I began to chase the red smoke signal; last night I heard gunfire and made my way toward that. Then I found these tents."

"Why are you so filthy? We spent the same amount of time in the swamp and didn't manage to get as muddy as you have."

"I did this to myself, because of those snakes," he replied. "I knew there had to be a reason for Wen-Jin's survival in this place, and for her to be that dirty was completely out of character. I figured those two facts had to be connected so I covered myself in mud, the way she had. Once I did that, the snakes couldn't see me. It's because they're attracted to heat and the mud kept my body cool."

Suddenly my spirits rose—this tactic might ensure our survival. At least we could keep going without fear of the damned reptiles that stalked us. I told Qilin what we had gone through since we were last together and he listened without comment.

"I'm so glad you're back," I concluded. "Panzi can't travel for a while and Fats and I are whipped. If we don't rest, we're going to die. But one more person makes it easier for us to keep watch, and to move on when the time comes."

He glanced at me and said, "In a place like this, one more or one less makes no difference." He turned to the nearest pool and began to scrub off his covering of mud.

When he was clean, he sat with his eyes closed, unreachable as always.

I took a bath and then went to check on Panzi. He was still in a feverish, restless sleep and Fats hadn't stirred for hours. Clearly I wasn't released from guard duty.

When Fats awoke in late afternoon, he stared at Qilin and gasped, "Holy shit, what dream is this? Don't wake me up, please." He spat and I saw blood on the ground. "You're hurt, fat man. Take it easy."

I handed him a cigarette and told him Qilin's story. He shuddered. "I dreamed about snakes crawling all over me the whole time I was asleep. Maybe we don't need to worry about them anymore."

"My turn to dream about horrors to come," I said and immediately drifted off. It was evening when I awoke; I smelled food cooking and remembered that Fats was quite the chef. I tried to move but my muscles screamed in protest. As I tried to get to my feet, I heard Fats say, "We can't let Young Wu know about this; he'll go crazy if we tell him."

CHAPTER SEVEN

UNCLE THREE'S MESSAGE

Fats fell silent when he heard me get up. Then he called, "Get over here. We saved you some dinner—eat it before it turns cold."

"You can't distract me with food, you bastard. What did you just say? What can't you let me know? We've had enough secrets—no more, damn it."

"You were still asleep when you heard me and misunderstood my words. I said we couldn't let you get so tired again or you'd lose your mind with exhaustion."

"You're a bad liar, Fats. Don't try to imitate my uncle—you're not in his league. Tell me what's going on here or I swear I'll choke it out of you."

Fats glanced at Qilin, sighed, and said, "Follow me and look at this thing."

I could barely walk, but Fats supported me as we approached the canopy where the documents were kept. He picked up the papers, uncovering the stone platform beneath, and gestured toward writing, scrawled on the rock in charcoal:

"We've already found the entrance to the Palace of the Queen of the West. Once we go inside, there will be no return, so this is goodbye. It's what I wanted and I have no regrets. This place is dangerous. You must leave as quickly as possible."

As I stared at the words in shock, Fats said, "I saw this when we first arrived and I covered it with the documents so you wouldn't see it. It looks like your uncle has gone forever, Young Wu."

It was beyond a doubt my uncle's careless scrawl. I kept looking at his writing, feeling nothing at all. Is this what Qilin feels all the time, I asked myself, no fear, no anger, no sorrow?

Now I knew there was no need to worry about my uncle, only myself. The knowledge was calming and for the first time in ages I felt at peace. I didn't even care about answers to this gigantic mystery; with Uncle Three gone, this no longer had anything to do with me.

Fats pulled me back to our campfire and handed me a plate of food. I looked at it with no appetite as he said, "You mustn't worry, Young Wu. Your uncle may find his way back to you someday. He's done it before."

"I don't care," I told him. "I'm just wondering where to find that entrance he wrote about. It can't be too far away."

"Why don't we go look for clues later? Maybe we'll find something," Fats replied. He turned toward Qilin who responded, "The only reason why Wu Sansheng left this message for us is because he's certain we'll never be able to find this place."

"Why not?" Fats asked.

Staring into the bonfire, Qilin answered, "Wu Sansheng is intelligent and calculating. He knows that we'll figure out that the entrance is nearby after we read these words. He doesn't want Young Wu to take any chances, so if the entrance were easy to find, he wouldn't have left any message at all. The fact that he did indicates that this entrance must be extremely difficult to find, and even if we found it, we'd never discover how to get inside."

He had a point. I sighed and thought that if there had been any clues at all, Uncle Three would have destroyed them just to keep me from following him.

"Then we came here for nothing?"

Qilin shook his head. "For you guys, this is probably a good thing."

"I've come hundreds of miles through the Gobi Desert and a jungle to get here. So you say turning back with nothing more to carry with me than a sunburn is a good thing?" Fats scratched his head as he leaned against a rock. "There's nothing here, not even broken objects. What a waste of time and energy this trip has been."

"But it's not a proven fact that this entrance is impossible to find," Qilin continued. "There's something really wrong with this campsite. It doesn't look like a simple retreat took place here. There could be more to your uncle's message than you think. Look at all of the backpacks these men left behind; it's obvious this group didn't even think about getting their gear together. It's as though they were fleeing from something, without thought or planning. And if they were going into a place they would never leave, Wu Sansheng certainly wouldn't tell his men that. He must have written this message at the very last moment after everyone else had set off. If his men had seen it, would they have been willing to go off to die?"

"This is fucking weird," Fats interrupted. "We need to think this through before we go off into the jungle again. Let's look at what we know for sure. Look at this message. It had to be written by your uncle after all the men had gone. Now let's consider that those men might have taken their backpacks, because they were planning on staying alive—and yet there are so many packs still here. This means only one thing to me—the men who carried those backpacks were no longer alive. And they died after they set up this campsite and before it was abandoned. But there's no sign of death here so it happened somewhere close by. The question is did they find the entrance before these deaths or after?"

"Could the snakes have killed so many men?" I quavered, suddenly feeling something and wishing I had stayed numb instead.

"Don't worry. When you were sleeping, this guy and I got enough buckets of mud to keep us all safe," Fats reassured me. "We're going to cover our tents with mud as well as our bodies. But this place feels evil—who knows what else is hanging around here. And we're well aware that the swamp comes alive at night—we have to be especially vigilant now that it's dark."

"I'll take the first watch since I just woke up," I said but Qilin overruled me. "No, this is my job. Get some more rest."

"We'll both do it," Fats told him. "I'll sleep until midnight and then join you. You know my eyesight is pretty damned good. Tomorrow we can look for a better place to camp and perhaps we can all rest—then look for that entrance. What do you say?"

"No," Qilin said, "first we have to find Wen-Jin."

Fats and I exchanged glances, both of us speechless. But Fats wasn't a man to stay that way for long. "You might as well say we'll go and rescue this guy's Uncle Three. It makes as much sense—and who's to say whether Wen-Jin even knows where the entrance is? She never mentioned it in the notebook

Young Wu found."

"Oh, she knows about it. Just call it a hunch I have."

"I have a hunch of my own," Fats scoffed. "My hunch is this whole trip is a goose chase."

"Hold on, Fats," I said, "I think Qilin's right. We found out about this because of those videotapes sent to Jude Kao's team and to me. They led us to discover that Wen-Jin had made this expedition years ago and sent us in the same direction. She sent the tapes; she wanted us to come here. Why? My uncle probably has some information that we don't, given to him by the remnants of Ning's group, but it was no doubt limited. Only Wen-Jin has the whole picture. And besides, I want to find out whose face was on that videotape—that guy who looked like me. I want to ask Wen-Jin about that, as trivial as it may seem to you. We need to capture her and get some answers. Maybe we can figure out a trap and lure her into it."

"With what? Our seductive bodies? We're the answer to a woman's prayers, I'm sure," Fats sneered.

"Oh shut up, Fats. We need to understand why she's running from us in the first place. After all, she's the one who wanted us to come here. She said she was waiting for us. Has she gone mad in this place?"

"No," Qilin said slowly. "She has a good reason to run. She's afraid—but maybe not of us. She showed herself to us and she didn't need to do that. But something made her run."

My entire body turned to ice. "*It*—in her journal she wrote of running from '*It*' and she had sent a message that '*It*' was traveling with us when we were with Ning's group. Did she see *It* when she came to us in the swamp? Is that what made her disappear?"

"Yes," Qilin said.

I immediately looked over at Fats and then toward Panzi lying in the tent. I looked at Qilin and thought I was losing my mind.

"She saw you, Young Wu, me, and Panzi. So that means it was one of us who scared her away? Which one of us is the bad guy here?"

Neither Qilin nor I said a thing. Fats raised his arm. "I'm a good guy. It's definitely not me."

"It's just a theory, Fats. Don't get hysterical. We've all worked to save each other. I'd rather think Wen-Jin was hallucinating for some reason," I muttered.

"The key problem is—what in the end is *It*?" Fats asked. "Do you know, Qilin?"

Qilin looked up at him and shook his head.

"Could someone have disguised himself as one of us, so one of us is actually an imposter?" Fats asked as he pulled his thick skin on his face to prove his innocence. "You see, my skin is real."

"I thought about this already. When you were sleeping, I checked you and Panzi," said Qilin. "You guys are no problem there."

I recalled the moment when I found him squatting next to Panzi. So that was what he was doing. It seemed as though this idea had been in his mind for quite some time; this guy was well ahead of the game.

Fats looked at me and said, "What about Young Wu?"

I pinched my face. "Don't worry. I'm absolutely real."

"That's hard to say. You joined us halfway on the road. Perhaps you're the imposter. Come over and let me check you out," Fats said. He reached over and pinched my face so hard that tears sprang to my eyes before he let go. Then he said,

"Okay. You passed."

"So it's probably not us that made her run." Qilin pointed to Wen-Jin's journal in my pocket and asked, "Is there any relevant information in that?"

I took it out, turned the pages, and shook my head. "It tells us only that 'It' has a certain level of intelligence. I think It's a human being, but I don't know why she refers to It as she does."

Fats stood up. "Speaking of that, isn't it your Uncle Three who's tracking her down? Could It be your Uncle Three? The night was so dark it was almost pitch-black. Perhaps Wen-Jin made a mistake. Don't you look a bit like your uncle, Young Wu?"

"I'm much more handsome than my uncle," I protested but as I spoke, Fats leaned over, grabbed Qilin's cheek, and pulled it hard. Then he sat back, looking embarrassed. "So you're as innocent as the rest of us—can't blame me for wanting to be sure."

As usual, Qilin had no reaction to the attack. Fats shrugged and went on, "Maybe It isn't a living thing but something completely different. Perhaps It's something we're carrying with us."

Qilin frowned. "Wait a second. Speaking of nonliving objects, we forgot something."

"What?" Fats and I leaned closer.

"Ning."

"You mean her corpse? Why would Wen-Jin care about that? They never met."

Fats clapped his hands together and said, "Aiya, Young Wu! Don't you remember what we found in the forest last night? Could there have been something wrong with Ning, so that after she died, she became that monster?"

"How the hell do I know? We can't solve this by making random guesses. We didn't see whatever it was—why decide it was Ning? It makes more sense to stop concocting ghost stories and decide how to trap Wen-Jin."

Fats yawned. "I've already decided that's impossible. My question is how we're going to make it through the night. Where's that mud?" He walked to a bucket and began daubing mud all over Panzi's tent; I went to help him. Then I checked on Panzi, smearing him with mud too. His temperature was normal and he was sleeping calmly at last.

We searched the camp for weapons. There were none so Fats collected an arsenal of heavy stones, along with pieces of wood to use as torches. Setting them ablaze, he placed them around the campsite, just as the fog began to roll in again. Soon our site was shrouded in mist, making it impossible for us to see what lay beyond our tents.

Tonight the fog had an eerie blue tint that hadn't appeared the night before. I began to remember stories of poisonous swamp vapors carried in the night air, and I grabbed Fats by the arm. "Maybe we should look for gas masks. That fog could hold a miasma that might kill us all."

"You think too much, Young Wu. There was no poison last night and logic tells us this fog came from the same place. Stop worrying, damn it, and get some rest. Let Qilin and me do the thinking for a change."

I went into Panzi's tent and tried to sleep but only dozed lightly. I became fully conscious when I realized I had to pee. I raised my tent flap and was faced with complete darkness. The campfire and all of the torches had gone out.

CHAPTER EIGHT

BLIND

Quickly I dodged back into my tent, wondering what the hell had happened. In my semiconsciousness I'd heard nothing. Where were Fats and Qilin?

There was no sound of anybody outside. I groped for my flashlight and turned it on. The battery was dead. I pulled my cigarette lighter from my pocket. There was no flame when I struck it, not even a spark of light, but as I held it, it grew hot, burning my fingers. I dropped it. The damned thing had ignited but emitted no light.

I was in absolute darkness, as if something had covered my eyes. Not even the fluorescent numbers on my watch were visible in the blackness that surrounded me. I couldn't see my own hand in front of my face. What had swallowed up all of the light?

Then I fell into a panic. Had I gone blind? I began to rub my eyes, blinking them violently. Still I could see nothing. I crawled to Panzi's side, feeling grateful he was still there. His body was burning with fever again and I didn't try to wake him.

Where were the others? Why couldn't I hear them? I crawled to the edge of my tent and called softly into the night. Nobody answered. Why didn't they hear me? Fats might have fallen asleep, but Qilin? Never.

Something happened to them, I thought, maybe the same thing that had happened to the missing men in my uncle's group. Had they gone blind too and stumbled away from the camp? Did camping in this place cause men to lose their eyesight? Who could survive in this place without being able to see? It was a way to commit murder without touching the victim. In my case, I'd probably expire because I was scared to death; I'd always been afraid of the dark.

Out of the night came a sound, an unfamiliar, unintelligible voice. Slowly I recognized it—it was that weird static-ridden radio transmission of the night before. Could it be Ning? Was it her ghost haunting me? Whatever the sound was, it came accompanied by snakes—so they had to be nearby too. Was my tent flap closed?

I groped to make sure that it was and as I did, something burst in toward me, almost knocking me over. A hand pressed over my face, a fat hand holding something that I realized was a gas mask. I reached out and put the mask over my nose and mouth as Fats spoke, "You were right. The mist is poisonous. Once you have the mask on, you'll be able to see again in a minute. But be quiet—there are snakes everywhere in the camp."

"Where did you guys go just now?"

"Son, it's a long story," Fats answered. "Do you think it's easy to find gas masks in the dark?" He was interrupted by the sounds of static and murmured, "Shut up." He pushed a knife into my hand and moved away. I grabbed his arm and he hissed, "A snake bit Qilin and I have to take care of him. Stay here until you can see again."

I sat in terror. What if Fats was attacked too? Panzi and I would never survive on our own. I clutched my knife and waited for the blindness to lift, wondering if Fats had given me a weapon for self-defense or suicide. I began to shake uncontrollably and curled up into a ball, listening to the intermittent static outside. Slowly a mist formed before me. The blackness turned to gray and slowly lightened. I could see edges and shapes emerge in the beam of my flashlight. I still couldn't see the doorway of my tent but there was something moving in front of me, a vague shadow. Thinking it was only my imagination, I ignored it and went over to Panzi. His temperature had returned to normal and I wondered how his fever had gone down so quickly.

Still without full vision, I groped for my canteen so I could give him a few sips of water. I turned to feel behind me and a shadow flashed before me again, a shape with arms and legs. If it were Fats or Qilin, they would say something, I realized. Quietly I called out, "Who's there?"

The shadow darted into the farthest corner of the tent and began to move quickly. My vision slowly allowed me to see that whoever was there was rummaging through a backpack. A swampy odor filled the air and I knew the figure, like the rest of us, was daubed with mud. I moved closer, hoping to get a better look, but I was too slow. In a second the figure was gone, leaving me to wonder if it had been real.

Lights approached the tent, along with the sound of footsteps, and Fats's voice rasped, "Turn off your flashlight, now!" As I did, he whispered, "Lie down and no matter what happens, don't make a sound."

I hit the floor of the tent and heard Fats breathing beside me—then an explosive noise erupted as though something had hit the wall of the tent next to us. I heard it again and again—then the crack of tent poles and the whooshing sound of a collapsing tent filled the darkness. Something outside had just demolished the tent closest to us.

Our own tent began to shake. I covered my head with my arms, knowing we were going to die, but the motion stopped and I heard the crashing sounds move away to a far corner of our campsite. I could hear more tents fall to the ground—at least a dozen of them—as the noise continued for half an hour. It was like listening to an earthquake.

Everything went silent and when I sat up, I found I could see again. There were Fats and Qilin, covered in mud, looking as though they'd just come out of a pigpen. Qilin was clutching his wrist and Fats was covered with spots of blood.

We didn't dare to speak. After waiting a while, Fats slowly opened the tent flap and daylight flooded in. We stepped outside into early morning. Our campsite looked as though it had been hit by a tornado; our tent was the only one still standing. As Fats and I stared at the damage, a thud sounded behind us. Qilin had fallen to the ground.

CHAPTER NINE
THE TEMPLE WALLS

We picked him up and carried him back into the tent. He had two small puncture marks on his wrist but they weren't deep. "He shook off the snake the minute its fangs touched his skin, but his hand had already turned blue," Fats told me. "He tied his belt around his arm, sucked out as much venom as he could, and cut a cross on the bite to bleed out the rest of the poison, but he wasn't quick enough to prevent some of the venom from entering his system. We had one hell of a night out there."

I injected a shot of serum as an antidote and then checked his hand for swelling. It was just a bit puffy and I was certain that if we kept Qilin quiet, he'd overcome whatever poison had felled him in his tracks.

"Tell me everything that happened to you last night," I demanded.

"When we began to lose our vision, I remembered your theory that the fog was toxic so I ran off to find some gas masks. Qilin soaked a couple of towels in muddy water, which helped ward off the mist, but by the time I finally found some masks, I was nearly blind. Qilin wasn't much better off. When a snake lunged out of the fog, he didn't see it until just before it struck. He grabbed the back of its head and tossed it aside, but it was too late. He did what he could as I already told you. Then I heard you calling for us. I brought you a gas mask and then came back to help Qilin.

"As I ran to him, I saw the snakes, a huge number of them, all coiled together and swiftly moving in unison, like a massive school of fish swimming through the ocean. Together they hurled in one wave to destroy the tents, with the force of a goddamned tsunami—come to think of it, that's probably how they carried off Ning's corpse. Because we had covered this tent with mud, they couldn't see where we were, but they knew we were here somewhere. Turning the camp to rubble was their way of making sure we'll have to get out of here—and they'll be ready for us when we do. Thanks to Qilin and his mud trick, we may outwit them still.

"We can't stay here," he continued. "They'll come back for us after dark. Can you see clearly now?"

I nodded and he said, "Good. We have to pack everything that we can use and leave by afternoon. Somehow we have to carry these two and cover some ground at the same time. Take a short rest—we both need it—and then we'll get to work."

After a brief nap, we started rummaging through the damaged tents to salvage what we could: packaged food, bottles of water, flashlights, and fuel canisters for our camp stoves. By the time we packed the supplies, it was already noon. Both Panzi and Qilin were in bad shape. Panzi was still unconscious and Qilin was awake but very weak. The swelling in his hand had gone down, which was a good sign, but he was too feeble to walk.

His mind was still sharp. We explained what our plan was and he shook his head. "You won't get far with the two of us. Go inside the temple, as far from the water as you can manage," he gasped.

"He's right, "Fats said. "The water that flows into the pools comes from the swamp. That's how the snakes entered our camp, through the drainage holes that feed the pools."

Cautiously we set off with our supplies, through a window and down a hallway of the temple. The interior was huge and airy, with two floors but no stairway between them—or at least none that we could see. The interior walls had collapsed, forming a steep mound of rock that would get us to the upper floor. We scrambled up and found a large room with walls of stone that were still intact. From there we could see the campground and the surrounding area.

"A good vantage point," Fats said, and we brought up our gear. Then we went back for the other guys; Qilin was almost strong enough to walk on his own, which was good because carrying Panzi was like transporting a tractor.

The sun's fierce glare began to dwindle rapidly and we knew dusk was on its way. As I watched the trees below turn into dark and threatening shadows, pressure tightened around me like a vise around a wooden plank. Could we survive another night in this place?

"Hurry," Fats broke into my black mood. "We need to bring up some buckets of mud, in case those snakes find us again."

We scrambled to get into our protective covering and made a cold meal, not wanting to send out a large amount of smoke that might let the snakes know where we were. Fats made a small fire with charcoal to keep away mosquitoes and there we sat, waiting for the fog to roll in, all of us silent and lost in our private thoughts.

Fats of course could never stay speechless for long and I heard him ask, "What in hell are you up to?" I looked over and saw that Qilin was rubbing the stone wall. As usual, he made no response, so I went to see what he was doing.

As I came close, he muttered, "I found it." He had uncovered some carvings in the stone by rubbing them with charcoal. "Look," he explained. "You can't see them in daylight. They're only visible if you bring them out with charcoal—see?" He rubbed charcoal on a portion of the wall and more carvings appeared, their shapes clearly visible—serpents writhing in the rock as though they were alive.

Under the charcoal in Qilin's restless hands, more and more carvings emerged until the room was full of reptiles, looking as though they were struggling to break free from the wall that held them.

"This tells the story of the snakes," he said, swaying unsteadily in the dim light of our small fire, "but I have to think about it before I can put it into words. So no questions please."

I did my best to puzzle out the meaning of the carvings on my own. I could see sacrifices and ceremonies in the stone, but none of this made sense to me. It looked as though people long ago may have worshipped these reptiles, which wasn't at all unusual. Snakes brought death and for a long time nobody understood the power of their venom. It was only known that a bite would kill, with just one small wound, and primitive people ascribed that to magical powers.

There were images of insects that looked like corpse-eating bugs, and the larvae that produced them were being eaten by the snakes. Why didn't the poison in the eggs kill the snakes? Who was more poisonous, these snakes or the corpse-eaters?

Qilin beckoned to me and I moved to his side, where there was a picture of a battle. "It's the people of the Empire of the Queen of the West," he said, "they're fighting a much more powerful army, men on horseback, while the queen's troops are all on foot. It looks like an invasion."

Then he stopped, looking puzzled. He touched the leader of the horsemen, a figure carried on a chariot, richly dressed. Slowly he stammered, "I—I know who this is. He's King Mu of Zhou."

King Mu was a legendary figure who had traveled to this part of the world and had been received hospitably and graciously by the Queen of the West. But not in these pictures—this was no diplomatic mission, this was carnage.

Then things got worse. The Zhou army rode up to the gates of the palace, which had stone towers like the ones we saw when we first entered this hellhole. The soldiers were greeted by women with the heads of snakes, who hurled some sort of liquid at the invaders from the tops of the towers. Then an army of snakes swarmed out over the palace walls, threw themselves on the army, and chased them from the area.

"It looks like King Mu invaded the empire, but was

repelled by the poisonous snakes. He concocted the story of the friendly reception to cover up his humiliation. These poisonous snakes were the guardians of the Empire of the Queen of the West. No wonder her people bred them and treated them as if they were gods." I stopped talking, feeling certain there was more to the story.

As I studied the bas-relief, it appeared to reveal that the stone towers we had seen protruding from the water were linked together and that the snakes were kept in the drainage tunnels beneath the city, where they were fed the heads of people who had been decapitated. How were they lured out at times when they were needed to defend the city from invasion? And how did these people come up with the idea of such superlative guards, every last one of them poisonous, lightning quick, and unstoppable once they had launched an attack?

So the snakes had been kept underground and emerged to the earth's surface when those who tended them had died out. But they still guarded the Empire of the Queen of the West, even though there was little left for them to protect.

Qilin called my attention to a huge carving of a mammoth serpent wrapped around an equally huge tree while smaller snakes coiled around the larger one.

"It's a python, like the one we killed, fighting with the smaller cockscomb snakes," I said.

"No," Qilin replied. "They're mating."

"But they're two different species," I argued.

"Don't horses and donkeys mate to make mules?" he asked. Then he stretched out his abnormally long fingers to touch the raised lines of the tree that the python had curled itself on. "Strange," he murmured. He grabbed more charcoal and uncovered more of the wall before him, revealing the entire carving. What looked like a tree was actually a monstrous basilisk, the most gigantic of all serpents, the size of a locomotive. It made the python look as insignificant as a hairpin, with the cockscomb snakes as flimsy as a bunch of toothpicks.

"Now I understand," Qilin said slowly. "The cockscomb snakes are only supporting the python, to keep it from slipping to the ground. It's the basilisk and the python that are mating."

I traced the lines of the smaller snakes; they were all wrapped together in a massive union of strength. "So that's what Fats saw," I said. "They form a social group the way ants do; is this basilisk their queen?"

"The mother serpent," Qilin replied. "The python is her male consort. We saw the python; is the basilisk still alive somewhere in this place?"

"The largest snake I ever heard of was an anaconda that was 160 feet long. Snakes have no fixed life span. They die when they're too large to hunt down prey. But what if other snakes brought food to a gigantic reptile; how long could it stay alive then?" I shuddered at the thought of this basilisk breathing somewhere near us. "But this carving has to be three or four thousand years old. No snake could live that long."

The carvings that followed this one showed people bowing before a snake that stood on end in front of a crowd, confirming the theory that reptiles were worshipped in this kingdom. Beyond that image, there were no more carvings.

9. THE TEMPLE WALLS

We went back to the fire and told Fats what we had found. "So that's what became of Ning's body," he said, "but if the basilisk is dead, what are the smaller snakes bringing the bodies to? What's being fed?"

"Perhaps they're working for the pythons. If there were still a basilisk, certainly we would have seen some trace of it by now," I suggested.

"I feel better now that I understand why these damned things do what they do. It's instinct, not evil genius," Fats said. "But they're still a hazard and we still have to outwit them somehow. Let's hope the mud continues to throw them off our track."

"I'm confused about the shadow I saw in the tent last night. Did you two see anything like that?"

"No, it was probably a trick of the light as your vision came back to you," Fats told me, but Qilin looked up with a startled expression in his eyes. "You saw a shadow rummaging through a backpack? That was Wen-Jin."

He stood up, said "Follow me," and ran out of the temple with me at his heels.

CHAPTER TEN

THE HUNTERS AND THE HUNTED

Qilin led me back to our old tent, where he grabbed a waterproof bag, two cups, and a large flashlight, then raced into the jungle, with me stumbling behind. He came to the edge of the swamp, scooped up cupfuls of mud, and smeared his body with it. He poured cups of mud over my head and shoulders until we both looked like Wen-Jin when we first saw her.

"What do you plan to do?" I asked and he replied, "We're going to catch Wen-Jin. She's looking for food, she must be starving, and we're going to set a trap to capture her when she comes out tonight."

"Tonight? Forget it. I'm not going to wait here after dark for anyone."

"Then why did you come here at all?"

I froze as Qilin gave me a blank, cold gaze and walked away without looking back.

Thoughts torrented through my brain. Why stare at me like that? I came only because every one of you is hiding the truth from me. That's why the hell I had to come here. What other choice—

All of a sudden I got his point. It was too late to be scared of dying. "Shit," I muttered and got up to follow him.

We went back to tell Fats what we intended to do; he was a bit hesitant at first but soon agreed. "She's not stupid," he said. "She'll probably come out as soon as the sun goes down, before the mist rises. Here's some food to lure her to you."

Qilin smeared fresh mud all over Panzi, then turned to Fats. "We need you to go too," Qilin told him. "We'll be back to take care of Panzi before the fog hits."

We walked back to the tent, put the food next to it, and hid in the shadow of our ruined tents, watching the sun sink below the treetops. We strained to hear any sort of sound, keeping completely motionless and silent under our armor of mud. Suddenly a figure came slowly out of the jungle; it was a woman.

"I'm going straight toward her. You two come in from each side," Qilin breathed. We heard rustlings from the bags of food but Qilin remained still for a few minutes. Then he lunged forward; we heard a scream and the sound of running footsteps. Fats and I raced out on opposite sides; we all three converged upon her at the same time.

Wen-Jin ran in a circle, looking terrified. She looked so young, no more than eighteen, and much prettier than she had been in her photo. My heart went out to her immediately and I called, "Don't be afraid, Auntie."

She ran toward me and I held out my arms in welcome, but she ducked, grabbed me, and knocked me to the ground. Then she sprinted into the rising mist, with Fats and Qilin close behind. Cursing my stupidity, I followed.

Wen-Jin was far ahead and I could no longer see her. Instead I was chasing a dim view of Fats's back. We ran out of the campsite to a broad, flat area just before the beginning of the jungle. Qilin cornered her near a boulder and we all closed in.

"Lady, what the hell are you afraid of?" Fats asked. "We're good guys. Stop running and let's relax."

Wen-Jin's only answer was a muffled cry as she sprang onto the rock like a trained martial arts practitioner. Qilin leaped up and grabbed her. She struggled, and both of them landed in the swamp water below.

Fats and I ran after them and saw the same kind of deep, bottomless pool that was near the temple. Qilin came up to the surface alone. "I had to release her," he sputtered, "or she might have suffocated in my grip." We waited at the pool's edge to grab her as she surfaced, but Wen-Jin stayed underwater.

Could she have drowned because she didn't know how to swim? Had we killed her? Qilin dived back into the pool to look and came up empty-handed. "There are drainage tunnels leading out of that pool—she must have escaped through one of them."

"What should we do? Won't the snakes find her? We've got to get her out right now!" I said. I stopped as I heard the sounds of someone splashing out of the water, panting heavily somewhere behind us.

We rushed toward the noise and saw another pool, with wet footprints leading from it into the jungle. We followed the trail hastily and soon heard the pad of footsteps and gasps of rapid breathing. We sped up only to be engulfed in darkness—Wen-Jin had led us back into the trees.

I hesitated for a second and in that instant Fats and Qilin disappeared from view. I could dimly hear footsteps in the brush but couldn't make out where the sounds were coming from. I was completely disoriented and awash with panic. I ran blindly toward where I thought I heard rustling leaves and gasps for breath. I called out and a voice answered from behind me, a soft, nasal voice saying, "Young Master Wu?"

The fog was thick and I could see nothing but vines. "Wen-Jin, is that you?" I asked, my skin prickling with apprehension. Again she called my name and I sent my flashlight in the direction of her voice. There was nobody there—at least nobody I could see.

"Who's there?" I shouted. Still there was no answer and I swept the flashlight through the darkness again. "Are you part of Master Three's group?" I called.

"Young Master Wu?" the voice repeated. Now it came from my left, and I shone my light in that direction. There was nobody there.

"That's me," I answered. "Come out and show yourself. I'm a human being, not a ghost." I began to walk toward the voice again, but all I found was a large tree. From behind me, the voice called my name again and I shouted, "I'm right here."

A bush behind the tree began to shake. I rushed toward it, and stepped into empty air. I only realized I'd been lured to the edge of a cliff when I plunged over the side, rocketed to the bottom, and landed in a quagmire.

CHAPTER ELEVEN
THE RIVER OF CORPSES

If I had to fall off a cliff, at least landing in water, mud, and soft, spongy vegetation was the way to go. I had ended up in a fast-moving stream. Who was it who had lured me to the edge of nowhere and why did the jungle end so abruptly at that spot?

I swam to the bottom of the cliff and grabbed a rock that protruded from it. I'd lost my flashlight; I could see it halfway up the rock wall, still alight. I tried to climb up to it but the cliff wall was smooth and slippery; quickly I realized this was impossible.

I thought about looking for a better spot to make my ascent but I could only move with the current of the stream, and its unusual swiftness told me that a waterfall was probably its destination. So far I was still unhurt and I wanted to stay that way. My only choice was to wait for daylight and hope that Fats and Qilin would find me. I shouted until my throat was sore but no other voice broke the terrible silence—not even the mysterious voice that had called my name.

I checked my watch, grateful for the light of its fluorescent dial—several more hours until dawn. Sitting on my rock, I felt chilly. Both of my feet were in the water and I began to worry about the leeches Panzi had warned me against, but there was no other place to put my feet. I groped about, trying to find a rock or a submerged log to stand on. As I moved, I felt something underfoot—something that felt bristly, like fur or human hair. I moved away and the soles of my feet touched something soft. I reached down to touch whatever it was, then plunged my watch underwater, hoping its glow would show me what was there.

Beneath that vague light, I could see a body, a man's body, buried in the mud at my feet, his head clearly visible, his hair waving in the current like seaweed. I moved my arm and the light from my watch revealed a number of bodies, their arms laced together as though their comradeship had continued into death.

I tugged at the body that was closest to me; it felt as though it was weighted with lead. Then I saw hanging from his belt the same sort of gear that Fats and Panzi carried. His clothing was what they had been wearing when they rescued me in the City of Wind Ghosts. I had found part of my Uncle Three's group.

Fighting nausea, I made myself examine the corpse; there was very little decomposition, so he had been dead for only a couple of days. His flesh had a slightly blue tinge, which made me think he had probably died from snake bites. Had the snakes carried these men to this bog after they had poisoned them? Was my uncle's body here? Had the voice that lured me here come from a ghost of one of these dead men?

I had to stop thinking. To distract myself I searched the pockets of the body and found a heavy, waterlogged wallet. I tossed it up to my flashlight, hoping it would knock my light free and send it down the cliff into my hands. I missed.

Then I took a flashlight from the corpse's belt and threw

that after the wallet. It hit my larger light and both slid down into the water. The smaller flashlight was carried away by the current, but I managed to salvage mine. Now I could examine my surroundings.

The bog I was in looked like a circular pool, with the stream flowing through it. At its edge, the water was shallow enough that I could walk upstream, passing many bodies as I traveled. My pathway stirred up the water and mud that covered the corpses, and I could see their necks. On each one, the skin had turned black with a green patch near the throat. In the middle of that green bruise were two black marks, looking the same as the bite that had killed Ning.

No wonder there had been no signs of violence at the abandoned campsite. These men had been killed by snakes, perhaps while they were asleep or maybe when they had walked through the jungle. I forced myself to search their faces, looking for Uncle Three. All of them were so obscured by mud that it was difficult for me to make out any distinguishing features.

As I was about to give up, my miner's lamp shone on a face that wasn't completely covered with mud; it looked familiar and then I knew—it was Ning.

I choked and almost vomited. How did those damned snakes bring her body so far from where we had carried it? Was this place their food cache? Was a giant python on its way here for breakfast? My thoughts rushed to mind like volleys of gunfire, with one thought taking precedence over all the rest: I had to get out of here fast.

I waved my flashlight through the air and saw some vines hanging from the cliff that stretched to the surface of the water. I swam to them and grabbed on tight, then reached into the stream and replenished the mud that had been washed from my body. Climbing up as quickly as I could, I reached a sturdy tree branch and scrambled to reach its trunk. Just as I was ready to climb onto it, I heard something splash in the stream below.

Shining my flashlight into the water, I saw a tangled mass of thin red tubes, like intestines—an intertwined unit of cockscomb snakes, coiling along in one huge lump. From the middle of them I could see a hand sticking out. Then a head emerged, and a very flabby neck. "Oh holy shit, Fats," I groaned. "What the hell have you gotten yourself into now?"

Fats wasn't struggling. He wasn't moving at all. He can't be dead—not Fats, I thought, watching hundreds of snakes pull his body to the edge of the cliff. They pushed him over the side and I heard a heavy plop as he landed in the bog below.

Peering from the leaves of my tree, I saw Fats lying motionless in the mud. If he were dead, I had no chance of survival; if he were still alive, I had to try to rescue him, as he had done for me in the past.

The snakes seemed to have disappeared and I cautiously made my way back down the vines. As I approached Fats, I saw half of his face was underwater and I began to tremble. I bent down and touched his throat; he had a pulse but it was very weak. Then I saw the bloody puncture wound on his throat—a snake had got him.

From that spot, close to a main artery, it would take only a short time for the venom to course through his bloodstream. When Ning was bitten on the throat, her death was almost immediate. Fats, on the other hand, was still breathing. What was the difference between them?

As I stared, I saw blood on Fats's clothing, but he had no

other injuries that would have caused him to bleed. Maybe when the snake sank its fangs into his throat, Fats managed to kill it with his machete. Perhaps the amount of venom released before the snake died was too slight to kill him. Maybe Fats had a chance of survival, if I could get him back up the cliff. If he stayed in the bog, the snakes were certain to discover that he wasn't yet dead—and they'd make damned sure to finish him off properly.

It was a hellish task to pull Fats toward the vines and to tie him to those green ropes with his belt. But when I tried to pull the vines up the cliff, his weight was too much for me. I threw the vines over a large tree branch and used that as a pulley, but the branch creaked ominously under Fats's weight. If we survive this, I'm putting you on a diet, damn you, I thought.

I recoated both of our bodies with mud and then began to tie the vines into a kind of harness that I could use to pull Fats up the cliff. As I worked, he choked, gagged, and vomited up a foul-smelling green liquid. Mixed within it were tiny red scales from the skin of a snake. I touched his stomach; it was even more distended than usual and it felt rock hard, as if he had swallowed an iron bar.

Quickly I began to push with all my strength on Fats's stomach and he vomited repeatedly, bringing up green slime, more red scales, a white cottonlike substance, and something that looked like giant larvae. It was horrible to watch and I almost began to vomit myself, but his breathing became less labored when his heaving was finally over.

I forced myself to look at what had come out of Fats's belly. Could these larvae be eggs hatched by one of the snakes? Did all of the corpses below harbor the next generation of murderous serpents? I kicked the eggs into the stream and watched them float away. I think I understand what's going on here, I thought, and the knowledge was far from comforting.

This bog was a hatchery and the corpses served as incubators for snake eggs. As the corpses decomposed, they gave off heat that provided just what the eggs needed to mature into snakes. Or, even worse, perhaps the victims weren't really dead, just paralyzed so they would warm the eggs with their natural body heat.

But now my main concern was getting Fats and myself up the cliff and away from this place. I finished fashioning the harness of vines and pulled it tight around Fats's torso. He was still unconscious so I was working with dead weight. This contraption had to hold him or we would both be trapped in this hellhole.

When everything was in place and ready to go, I beamed my flashlight into the marsh below. It was invisible; all I could see was a cloud of dark vapor rising up toward Fats and me. Then it parted slightly, letting me see that the muck and mud was moving, as though something was stirring it with a giant spoon. That fragment of vision was soon obscured by more rising vapor.

Was it toxic gas formed by rotting vegetation? Would it make me go blind, as the temple fog had the night before? My only hope was that it wouldn't reach the area where Fats and I were, but that was an impossible dream. It was steadily advancing in our direction. Quickly I tore off one of my shirtsleeves and used it to cover my nose and mouth, then used my other sleeve to make a gas mask for Fats. I had just tied the cloth around his face when the gas touched my feet and then wrapped around us like a thick shroud. My throat began to itch and I struggled to hold my breath.

The vapor had a strange scent and it looked as though it consisted of small solid particles. I tried to grab one, like a snowflake, but nothing remained in my fingers. Somehow I had the feeling that I had seen this cloud of black vapor before, and I knew in my gut that Fats and I were in very bad trouble. I could hear strange sounds from the marsh, heavy thuds, like the footsteps of a gigantic monster; when I peered down, my flashlight showed only a rippling circle on the water's surface below. Was something hatching down there? Was a snake searching for prey in the swamp? Was it a gargantuan fish, like the Siberian salmon that tried to gobble up Lao Yang and me near the bronze tree of death?

A small groan came from Fats and when I looked at him, I almost shrieked. Streams of blood flowed from his eyes, he was panting heavily, and when I touched him his skin felt like cold marble. Was it the vapor or the snake venom that had him in such bad shape?

I tried to bring him into a sitting position but as I moved, we both plunged forward and straight down into the muddy pool where the mysterious ripple waited for us. I floundered about, grabbing blindly in search of Fats, but we had stirred up a lot of mud in our diving disaster and it was impossible to see into the pool. What was even worse, I realized, was that I was caught in a current and was being swept downstream.

The current moved faster and faster. My head bumped hard against something made of stone, and then I was washed into a tunnel. My body bumped along a series of inclines that felt like steps in a staircase and I began to somersault repeatedly as the stream pushed me along a narrow passageway. The water roared around me and I braced myself for a waterfall. Again I fell through another tunnel opening. The current lost its force and I had control over my body once more.

I had kept a death grip on my flashlight and was grateful I had one that was waterproof. I beamed it into my surroundings and saw I was in an underground reservoir, with water cascading from shafts in the walls all around me. I felt like a cockroach that had been flushed down a toilet into a septic tank.

The water in the reservoir moved steadily toward a carving of an animal on the wall. It trickled into a gaping mouth that was almost completely blocked with branches and other debris. Something was hanging from one of the branches; it was Fats.

I swam over to him. His face was blue and his breathing and pulse were both almost still. I pulled his legs up onto a pile of branches and pushed hard on his stomach. He vomited up at least a gallon of muddy water and began to cough. I rubbed his chest as hard as I could but my strength wasn't what it had been. I had to get both Fats and myself out of the water and I had no idea how to do that.

I heaved myself up onto a pile of dead branches and squirmed higher with great difficulty. The walls of the reservoir had to afford some sort of toehold or we would never leave this place. I grabbed Fats and tugged him behind me with every bit of energy that I had left. There was a dry tunnel opposite from where we were. Carefully I put Fats on some sturdy branches and began to climb over to the tunnel.

Out of the corner of my eye, I saw a flicker of motion. Then a voice I'd never heard before calmly and clearly announced, "Time's up!"

11. THE RIVER OF CORPSES

CHAPTER TWELVE

THE PERSON IN THE FOG

I knew I wasn't hearing things; this was definitely a human voice. It had to be a survivor from my uncle's team. There couldn't be anybody else wandering around this swamp.

"Who's there?" I called. I waited a moment; there was no reply. Grabbing a stick, I made my way along the mass of tree branches. The voice rang out again, "Young Master Wu?"

Whoever this guy was, he knew my name. My whole body lightened with relief and I shouted back, "It's me. Where are you? Are you trapped? Let me help you."

"Young Master Wu?" the voice asked again from the depths.

"It's me! It's me!" I shouted, moving through the branches as fast as I could. I could see nobody, and the person had stopped speaking. Annoyed, I yelled, "God damn it! Who the hell is in there? And what are you doing? Say something so I can figure out where you are."

Still there was no reply; something was very wrong. Had this guy been bitten by a snake, or was he poisoned by the black swamp vapor? I had to find him. Digging through the branches, I made an opening in the spot where I'd heard the voice. Nobody was there.

"What's going on?" I shouted and my voice ricocheted off the walls of the reservoir. Before the echoes faded, I suddenly heard that faint, strange voice again. "Young Master Wu?"

It sounded so close. Quickly I turned around and saw a man lying flat on his stomach just like me, on the other side of the tangled branches. He stared at me coldly with blood-red eyes. My throat tightened and I stared back at him, too startled to blink.

But human beings can only do that so long. I began to blink, but the eyes that watched me never moved a millimeter; it was as though they had been frozen. And they were red from blood that oozed from their sockets, just as blood had just exuded from Fats's eyeballs.

I groped in my pockets for my waterproof tin of matches, lit several, and tossed them toward the face. It was horribly mutilated; its chin had been eaten away. This man was dead. So who in the hell had been calling my name?

I had to get out of here now and I had to take Fats with me. I reached down, grabbed both of his hands, and pulled as hard as I could. It was impossible to move him as much as an inch.

But the harness of vines that I had made earlier was still bound around his chest. I grabbed it and tugged; slowly Fats came toward me. Once he was securely on the pile of branches, I did my best to administer a primitive version of CPR.

I pressed on his chest for a couple of minutes. He coughed up more water and took a deep breath. But in a second or two his eyes rolled up into his head and his breathing became shallow again.

I looked at the bloody puncture marks in his neck. As long as that poison was in his body, Fats had no hope of staying alive. I opened the puncture marks with the knife that I'd securely attached to my belt and let the bad blood flow. Then I continued to press hard on his chest, hoping he would hang on.

Behind me, the voice called me again. When I whirled to look for its source, only the corpse was there. I stared at it as a large snake—much larger than the one that killed Ning—crawled from the bottom of the damaged face and moved onto the pile of branches. It was less than ten feet away from Fats and me, crawling toward us purposefully.

Fats was motionless so I figured he wasn't going to attract the snake's attention. As quietly as I could, I slipped back into the water. Looking back up, I saw the snake turn its focus to Fats; it had stopped near him and was poised as though it would soon strike.

I had nothing close at hand but water, so I splashed as much as I could up toward the snake. It drew back and flew at me like an arrow shot from a bowstring. I saw a red flash and in less than a second its satiny scales were coiled around my arm and shoulder. Its fangs were almost in my flesh. I screamed and hurled it into the water. As soon as it landed, it launched itself at me again, and as it came, a voice emerged from its body. "Young Master Wu?" it said.

CHAPTER THIRTEEN
THE VOICE OF THE SNAKE

Hearing the snake speak, I turned as motionless as a boulder.

I knew these reptiles were deadly, but no matter how evil they were, they couldn't possibly use human speech. Yet this voice just now was incredibly clear, and it seemed to come from the snake. I had to be hallucinating.

The snake kept its gaze upon me, as though it were trying to figure out why I didn't reply. It crawled closer, got up into my face, and once again said, "Young Master Wu?"

This time I heard it even more clearly and to make matters worse, I saw its jaws move as it spoke. It really was saying my name, and the damned thing had a Changsha accent. How could this be happening?

I remembered the voice that we heard calling me earlier; it had sounded exactly like what was coming from this snake, and neither voice said anything but "Young Master Wu." It was a parrot's voice, imitating only what it heard—and obviously it had heard Panzi calling me in his Changsha-accented Mandarin. But why was it parroting that phrase over and over? God damn it, I realized, it had been luring me and I fell into its trap. Now it was three inches away from my nose and I was only that far from death.

I leaned backward slowly; the snake followed my shift in position, keeping the three-inch distance between us. It could easily have attacked but it didn't. It seemed more important for it to keep me under its control, rather than kill me. What was it trying to do?

I stopped moving and as I stood motionless, something in the water struck me on the ankle. Bubbles began to form near me on the water's surface, and I rolled my eyes in that direction. In the pool was a white shadow with a human shape; whether it was dead or alive, I couldn't tell.

I watched without moving an eyelash as the bubbles formed a circle around me. The nearby tree roots began to tremble as though someone had grabbed their underwater tendrils. The snake turned and looked away from me, suddenly on the alert against an unseen danger. It raised its head, its skin turned bright scarlet, and it began to squawk like a chicken. I hoped it wasn't calling its tribe to come and help.

A hand grabbed my ankle and began to trace words upon my skin. The touch sent words into my brain—"Get ready."

Seeing nothing moving, the snake lowered its head, stopped squawking, and began to lose its bright red color as its body relaxed. The shadow below me floated upward and exploded from the water, grabbing the snake by its head. Startled, I slipped and fell into the pool. Not daring to look above the surface, I swam a safe distance away before turning my head back to where I had been.

The water frothed with violent splashing. A stream of red light sprang from the water, coiling around the branches on the bank and shrieking wildly. My rescuer called to me, "Hurry. Get out of here—it's calling for reinforcements," then dove from sight. I began to follow and then remembered Fats. I couldn't leave him to die. But when I looked over at the spot where I had left him, there was nobody there.

I called him, but all I could hear was the shrieking of the snake. Muttering, "I'm sorry, Fats," I swam after the mysterious figure, who led me into the mist and down a long tunnel that gradually held less and less water. Who was I following—a rescuer or another threat, a human or a ghost?

When we finally reached dry land, I didn't have the strength to pull my body into the dry part of the tunnel. I had just placed my hands on shore before realizing I didn't have the energy to hoist my body up. Wanting to cry but with no tears to shed, I groaned and slipped backward, the sounds of the shrieking snake coming closer. Someone grabbed me by the hand and pulled me to safety.

I was in a cave, next to someone who was wearing a gas mask. Behind were more people, also masked and carrying flashlights. One of them removed his mask and revealed a familiar face. It was my Uncle Three.

Before I could say a word, my uncle slapped my face hard and someone jammed a gas mask over my mouth and nose. Uncle Three replaced his own mask, barking out, "Carry him." Two men picked me up and everyone retreated deeper into the cave. An opening led us aboveground, where a few more people waited for us. And there, swaddled tightly and lying on a rock like a giant baby, was Fats.

CHAPTER FOURTEEN
THE ENTRANCE

I rushed over to Fats as soon as my carriers put me down. He was still unconscious, and someone was giving him an injection. "Fats, we are a couple of lucky bastards," I muttered before looking at the men who had saved us.

They were all wearing wet suits, as well as gas masks. The one suit that my rescuer had on was much older than the others and had faded to an ivory color, which is what had made the shadow in the water look so white. I knew I needed to thank this guy for saving my life and as I walked toward him, I saw the dark glint of sunglasses through the lenses of his gas mask.

"It's you," I yelped and he nodded. Before I could thank the Sunglasses Kid, my uncle came to my side. He stared at me for a minute and then sighed heavily. "Damn you, you little son of a bitch. Why don't you ever listen to me?"

I opened my mouth to reply but he gestured for me to shut up. In the Changsha dialect, he said, "Don't speak Mandarin. Where are Panzi and Qilin?"

I immediately told him everything we had gone through and Uncle Three responded, "Can't believe as clever as Fats is, he fell for this trick."

"What do you mean?"

"These snakes can imitate human speech. They mimic whatever they hear to lure you over the side of the cliff. We almost died because of that," one of the men said. "In this goddamned place, you can't believe your ears."

I glanced at Fats and asked Uncle Three, "Is he all right?"

"We've already given him an antidote. The rest is up to fate," Uncle Three said, looking at his watch. "Hurry up and take off your clothes."

"Take my clothes off? Why?" I hesitated and a few men tore my shirt from my back and stripped me of the rest of my clothing. They pressed me down against the rock and I heard someone say, "Damn it, those are really something."

I tried to turn and look at my back, but I was held so tightly that I couldn't move.

"Don't!" Uncle Three said softly. "Just stay still."

"What's on my back?" I struggled, feeling a surge of panic.

"Damn it. Stop fussing," my uncle told me. "You'll find out soon enough." Someone struck a match and the smell of sulfur hit my nostrils. I felt a wave of heat and the sensation of something moving on my back. Someone was crying, sounding horribly like a baby.

And before I had time to think about any of this, Uncle Three began to work on my back, poking me with something very hot. The strange cries grew louder and more miserable; whatever was on my back slid off.

"Get up and walk away quickly!" Without questioning the order, I struggled to my feet. My legs were numb, as though they'd fallen asleep, and I staggered as I tottered away from where I had been lying. I looked at my feet and saw some long, white, thin tubes clinging to my ankle. They looked like intestines; disgusted, I tried to kick them away. On the ground they began to move, showing tiny fangs as they opened their mouths and began to lunge at my leg.

Someone moved beside me. There was a flash of black light as a rock came crashing down, killing one of the baby snakes. More rocks hurtled near me, crushing the heads of the little reptiles, turning them all into a sticky paste at my feet. I could feel slime trickling down my back and I began to vomit.

A headless snake continued to writhe and wiggle; Uncle Three stabbed at it, cutting it in two. Then he handed me some clothes and said, "Wipe yourself clean before putting these on. Fasten your collar and pants legs."

"This...This...What's all this?" I stammered as I touched my back.

"These are newly hatched snakes. Their skin hasn't even hardened yet, or taken on any color. You were in the pool of corpses, and these little snakes hide there under the mud, attaching themselves to whatever passes by. Almost every one of us here has had them on our bodies," one of the men said. "When these snakes bite you, you feel a sharp pain, but then your back turns numb. You wouldn't feel anything even if you were lashed with a whip. Then they slowly drill their way into your skin, suck your blood, and when they grow up to the point that their poison can kill you, they'll come out of your skin. By that time, their bodies are engorged with blood, and their scales will have turned red."

I remembered feeling as if something was biting my

ankles when I was walking in the water. Could those snakes have crawled up and into me then? I touched my back again as I thought of this, and feeling the mucus, I vomited.

I wiped my back clean with my old clothes as another group of people came out from a shaft. One of them saw Uncle Three and shook his head as he whispered, "Master Three, we can't get out that way. What should we do?"

Uncle Three stood up, nodded, and replied, "We can't stay here any longer. We have to go back and return tomorrow. Let's get going."

Turning back to me, he muttered, "We'll discuss the rest of our concerns when we get back to our base. It's too dangerous here. Don't talk while we're walking, okay?"

I nodded. We immediately set off and made our way to the depths of the shaft.

I had no idea of where we were going. It was hard to see anything but I could hear familiar high-pitched clucking sounds nearby as we walked. Those snakes lived here, and they were everywhere around us.

We had walked for an hour or more when I heard a sound that I knew but couldn't identify. The temperature grew cooler and I could see moss-covered roots of living trees protrude through the rocks overhead. We seemed to be getting closer to the earth's surface and I tried not to feel too excited by this. I was more than ready to leave this subterranean maze of aqueducts that served as a giant snake nest. I wanted to see the sun again.

Finally we reached our destination. I could see an indistinct flame in the distance, and as we gradually approached the fire, I found that it was near a huge reservoir made up of six or seven terraced and connected ponds. There were columns and beams all around them, as if they were Roman bathing pools. After climbing down, I discovered a huge number of large, deep openings, like square holes on the rocky walls. They seemed to be connected to tunnels, forming corridors between caves.

The fire was within one of the caves. We walked toward its light, climbed some steps, and entered a spacious cavern that held a tent, some sleeping bags, and a lot of equipment. There were two people sitting there who were probably responsible for keeping the fire going. They had their backs to us and didn't seem to notice our arrival.

We were all exhausted from the journey, and I felt like I had almost no energy left in my legs. One of the men in our group kicked at the two guys who were tending the fire. "Get the hell up and give us some room to sit down, won't you? What are you doing, sitting there like logs of wood?"

The two men fell on their backs and stared up at us. Their faces were black and their eyes wide open. "Holy shit," I yelled. "They're dead."

CHAPTER FIFTEEN
THE REFUGE

I stepped away from the bodies, feeling as though I was going to puke again. Everybody around me broke into loud laughter and two of the men picked up the bodies, holding them in front of me. They were dummies, their diving suits stuffed with sand and their heads nothing more than inflated black plastic bags. Their eyes were made of chewing gum with pebbles in the middle to serve as pupils.

"We made them to fool the snakes but you fell for it too— we're better craftsmen than we thought," one of the guys hooted, and I joined in the laughter with complete relief.

"Are the snakes as easily fooled as I was?"

"As smart as they are, they can't tell the difference between a breathing human and a dummy. This helps too," the man said as he threw a smoke bomb in the fire. "Cover your nose, it's sulfur. Stinks like hell but it keeps the snakes away."

The Sunglasses Kid put some wood on the fire and went out to gather some more. We sat comfortably around the blaze and removed our gas masks. The man who had explained about the dummies sat near me and smiled. "My name's Mop, Young Master Wu. If you have more questions, I'll answer them if I can."

Before I could reply, my uncle sat next to me, handing me a

plate of food. I grinned at him and he barked, "What in hell are you smiling about? If you weren't my nephew, I'd have beaten the living shit out of you by now."

I hadn't seen Uncle Three look this good in months, not since we had set off for the cavern of the blood zombies. My smile grew broader as I looked at him. "Even if you beat me to death, I'd still pester you when I became a ghost. There's no way to get rid of me, Uncle. I'm with you, like it or not. Wouldn't you do the same if you were me?"

He lit a cigarette, took a deep puff, and then laughed. "Okay. I accept my fate. You're the same as your old man, damn it. You both look all soft and timid on the outside, but inside you're both the most determined bastards I've ever met. So you're here; there's nothing more to say. I can't turn you back out into the swamp, can I?"

"Okay, now tell me. What happened to you guys? How did you get ahead of us? Didn't Panzi say that you guys would wait outside the swamp for our signal?"

"Your uncle couldn't wait," the Sunglasses Kid broke in, sitting beside us. "He knew Wen-Jin was waiting for him here, and we only had so much time. How could we afford to wait for your signal?" He patted Uncle Three on his shoulders and continued, "Master Three, you're so sentimental. You didn't show such fidelity when we were singing karaoke with those girls in Changsha."

Uncle Three shoved his hand away and glared at him. "I was listening to that old lady saying that Wen-Jin was waiting for us ahead, and I realized this might be the last chance I'd ever get to see her again in my life. I couldn't miss this shot no matter what, or my whole life would have been lived in vain. To be honest, if I could just see Wen-Jin one more time, I'd be okay even if I died the second after we said hello to each other."

"Wait a second, you were listening to what old lady? Do you mean Dingzhu-Zhuoma? She passed the message on to you too?"

My uncle nodded. "I was only about ten hours behind you when Panzi led you toward this swamp. That old woman found me and gave me Wen-Jin's message—the same one she told Qilin and you earlier. I asked her for details; when she tried to be cute, I told her I'd cut her damned throat if she didn't tell me everything she knew. I tied up her grandson and her daughter-in-law and told her they were dead meat if she didn't start talking. Then she said that about a month after she had parted ways with the expedition, she ran into Wen-Jin again in Golmud. Wen-Jin seemed to be in trouble; she looked half-starved and frightened, as though she was hiding from someone. The old lady took her home and fed her. Later that evening Wen-Jin gave her the videotapes for safekeeping," Uncle Three said. "They didn't see each other again for ten years. Then a few months ago, out of nowhere, she received a letter from Wen-Jin asking her to send the videotapes to three different addresses. If any of the recipients showed up asking questions, she was told to deliver the message she gave to us.

"When I found out that Wen-Jin was alive and waiting at Tamu-Tuo, I almost went nuts. I set off right away and I guess I was traveling faster than you. I got ahead of you without knowing it and came into the swamp from another direction. We trekked through the rainforest overnight and set up camp inside the ruined buildings. I took some men to look for Wen-Jin the next night, but when we got back, all the other guys had disappeared. The next morning, we saw your signal, and I sent up the red smoke signal to keep you from danger; then we went to look for the missing men. We heard screams and followed the sound; of course they turned out to be the damned snakes—and we were lost in the swamp. We wandered around until we found you and Fats, but there was no sign of Wen-Jin."

I sat in silence after hearing this, trying to piece things together. The three people that Wen-Jin had mentioned in her journal were obviously me, Qilin, and Uncle Three. I had thought that Ning had been sent videotapes, but Qilin had been in her group and clearly he was the recipient. He passed them on to Ning so they could find Dingzhu-Zhuoma, hire her, and lay out the plan for this expedition. That would let Uncle Three distract Jude Kao and drain his resources by using them to find Wen-Jin.

"Uncle Three, since you were given the message, you must have been sent a videotape, right?"

Uncle Three looked at me, threw his cigarette into the bonfire, and nodded. "That's right. It had been sent to my shop in Hangzhou when we were still in Jilin. There was a big stack of mail waiting for me when I got home and I didn't find that package until I was back for a few days. Believe me, I didn't intentionally keep this from you."

I nodded. I believed him but something still troubled me. "Uncle Three, don't you think it's weird that Aunt Wen-Jin sent me videotapes? When you guys were together, I was just a little kid. I really can't figure out why and how she involved me in this whole thing. And that tape she sent Qilin was really disturbing—who was the person who looked like me, crawling like a madman on the floor?"

Uncle Three sighed and said, "No, it isn't weird at all. Wen-Jin had a good reason to send you the tapes."

CHAPTER SIXTEEN
MORE VIDEOTAPES

"Tell me the reason."

"Would you believe me if I did tell you?"

He looked at me as I fell silent, unsure of what to say or what to believe anymore. He laughed. "I've lied to you before because I had a reason so compelling that I had no other choice. I kept this up for as long as I could. I know you have no reason to believe anything that comes out of my mouth anymore so just wait a bit longer, won't you? Soon we'll find Wen-Jin and she can tell you everything."

"Uncle Three, I really don't want to wait any longer. Can't we just stop avoiding this issue? Please do as I ask for once."

Uncle Three lit another cigarette. After a moment of silence, he continued, "I've told you this many times. The whole thing is far too complicated, with so many secrets that I'm not even sure what it's all about in the end. So I feel sympathetic with what you're feeling right now."

Sympathetic my ass, I thought, no matter how little you know, you still know more than I do. Our positions are completely different. You're in the center of the whole thing, and I'm on the outside. I can't even find the door to get in.

But it wouldn't do any good to voice my thoughts. I didn't want to keep mulling over these things. I was here. Unless my uncle killed me, I was going to follow him all the way to the end, and then the secrets would come to light.

I drank a few sips of tea, rubbed my aching legs, and changed the subject. "All right, Uncle Three. What was on the videotape that Aunt Wen-Jin sent you?"

Uncle Three stood up, took his laptop from his luggage, and said, "I can't describe it. Watch it for yourself."

He flipped open the laptop screen and took out a disk.

"I asked one of my shop assistants to convert the video file to a DVD. It cost me three hundred bucks. I've watched it over and over again, but I still don't get it. So don't be too optimistic. The laptop battery's running down—make good use of what's left." He walked away but the Sunglasses Kid took his place, ready to watch with me. I wasn't crazy about having someone else in the audience but I shrugged and hit play.

The screen was dark with odd sounds, familiar but not recognizable at first. Then I knew—we were listening to the noise of running water. There was no light, no shadow; the only sign that we were watching a video was that sound of water, mixed with thunderclaps. Was that the sound of a waterfall crashing nearby? I wondered.

After about five minutes I heard people breathing and the sound of slow and stumbling footsteps on rock. Then they disappeared, leaving only the noise of water.

Clearly this tape was different. The others had been shot in the Golmud house; this seemed to be outdoors. Could it have been recorded here, when Wen-Jin's team first arrived ten years ago?

After twenty more minutes the water noises faded away and the footsteps returned, along with the sounds of birdsong and buzzing insects. A woman spoke. "Where are we? Have we gotten out yet?" She was panting and she sounded exhausted.

Nobody answered. It sounded as though things were being put on the ground, and the breathing grew heavier. Somebody coughed and then a man's voice asked, "Are there any cigarettes left?"

No one answered him; there was only a loud bang, like metal hitting the ground. The man who asked for cigarettes said, "Be careful."

Silence followed and the sounds of the water grew louder, but after a few minutes, the quietness resumed. The voice that had asked for cigarettes demanded, "Where in the hell are we going?"

Again there was no reply and I became impatient. I began to fast-forward the tape but the Sunglasses Kid grabbed my hand and stopped me. More words suddenly emerged from the tape; another man cried out, "Listen, the noises! Those things are coming again!"

A harsh whisper came from the first man. "No one make a sound!"

There was complete silence. Only the water could be heard, mingled with some other sound that seemed familiar. I leaned closer to the laptop, sure I had heard this somewhere else, and then I knew. I began to tremble and my mouth went dry. The noise came from the horn that I heard trumpeting loudly when Qilin had entered the giant bronze doors near the palace of doom.

CHAPTER SEVENTEEN

THE ASSEMBLY CALL

I'd never forget that trumpet call, the way it echoed as the bronze doors opened all by themselves to let Qilin enter with an army of the dead. Suddenly I wished Fats were with me right now to confirm what I heard drifting from my uncle's laptop. But even without him, I knew what I was listening to. It must have been recorded when Wen-Jin and her group approached the bronze doors and saw them open to allow an entrance to…what? A place that held such horror that Wen-Jin wrote nothing about it except for one terse sentence: "I have seen the Ultimate."

As I continued to listen, the horn gradually faded away, leaving only the sound of running water. Then the tape ended, giving me no answers, only more questions.

I listened to it one more time, hoping to catch something I'd missed, but my uncle was correct. There was nothing to be gained from this, other than the severe headache that throbbed in my temples after I switched off the computer.

The Sunglasses Kid grinned at me and moved away. Everyone else was either snoring or whispering, the fire was warm, and I began to relax. I couldn't sleep, even though I was thoroughly exhausted; the tape had me wide awake, my brain whirring uselessly.

I sat and tried to still my thoughts as my uncle moved toward me out of the shadows. His face was covered in mud; what I could see of it looked troubled.

"What do you think of what you just saw?" he asked me.

"I have no idea," I replied, "it certainly doesn't fit in with the other tapes at all. What have you been up to that's made you look like a crazy man?"

"One of the guys found something interesting over there in that trench. Go see for yourself."

I walked over and couldn't see a thing. There was a deep furrow in the rocky floor and at its bottom there was a crack in the surface, about the size of my body. My uncle joined me with the Sunglasses Kid and a few of the other guys. "Get in there," he ordered them, beckoning toward the fissure.

Then he shook his head. "Forget it. I'm going in myself and I'll take Four-eyes here with me. Lower us down on this rope."

As he and the Sunglasses Kid moved into the furrow, I grabbed Uncle Three by the arm. "You're going to run into snakes in there and when you do, that crack is too narrow to allow you an escape route. Can't you wait till daybreak?"

"As if daybreak's going to make a difference in this dark hole," my uncle scoffed. "We have our flashlights—don't be such a coward."

"Send some young guys in. Your old bones are in no condition to show off, damn it."

"I can take care of myself—I've been doing this long before you were born. I'm just going to take a look. I'll be right back up in just a few minutes."

He tossed a sulfur smoke bomb down into the bottom of the trench and grabbed two more, handing one to the Sunglasses

Kid. The other guys lowered the rope and the two of them slid down through the narrow opening into the darkness. Soon they reached the bottom and stood beside the fissure, peering into it with their flashlights.

The Sunglasses Kid looked up at us and made a signal that made the guys holding the rope curse when they saw it. "God damn it," one of them said, "they're going into that crack in the floor. The old man's gone nuts."

I was glad Panzi wasn't there; he would have killed this guy for his lack of respect, but the man would have died only for telling the truth. My uncle had gone right over the edge, in more ways than one. He had already disappeared into that narrow opening, with his companion following close behind. All I could see were gleams from their flashlights, dancing far below us.

We all held our breath and stood absolutely still, moving only after we heard my uncle yell, "Pull."

We all heaved on the rope, but only the Sunglasses Kid came up to the surface. "Your uncle wants you to go down there right now," he announced, staring straight at me.

Obviously my uncle was trying to kill me. I was the weakest guy in the bunch, and I was worn out from my earlier adventure with the snake and from rescuing Fats. I should have been flat on my back snoring right now and Uncle Three knew it. Either he wanted me dead or he had something important to show me. In either case, I had no choice; all the guys were staring at me, waiting for me to obey my crazy uncle.

"Come on, follow me," the Kid said, and he and I slid down the rope. It was a tight squeeze and I wondered how my uncle had managed to force himself through such a narrow opening.

We were surrounded by darkness that our flashlights

couldn't penetrate and the space was so narrow that I felt as though I couldn't breathe. I glanced at my companion who, of course, still wore his sunglasses.

"How can you see with those things on, anyway?"

He smiled. "I see better with them than without." That was his idea of an explanation. This kid had spent too much time with good old Poker-face.

The crack was as deep as it was narrow, as though someone had cut a mountain in half with a gigantic cleaver. There were small depressions in the wall that looked almost like shrines. Each one contained an object covered with dried, cracked mud, like a cocoon. As I looked around, I saw these depressions covering the wall of the fissure, as far as my eyes could see.

I reached out my hand to touch one and the Sunglasses Kid yelled, "Don't do that. Stop!"

"What's inside those things? What are they?"

"Dead bodies. This is a burial ground. Look through the crack and you'll see the bones of men buried in fetal positions. This is one of the world's earliest tomb sites, with graves of men who died while building this strange city." He waved and shouted into the darkness. "There's your uncle over there, waiting for us."

Another crack ran through the wall of our narrow passageway, and within it was my Uncle Three. He pulled me inside, where the space was even more constricting than where we had just been. The three of us hunched as low as we possibly could and I peered at the walls. They too had the same cocoon-filled shrines; I shuddered and pulled my body into a tight ball to keep from touching them.

"Why did you tell me to come down here?"

"I wanted you to look at this thing," my uncle replied and

gestured for me to follow him. Hunched over like deformed dwarfs, we walked farther into this opening.

He directed his flashlight toward a wall of sandstone behind a tangle of tree roots, where words were carved into the soft rock. It looked as though they were written in English, and I grabbed my uncle's flashlight to see what they said. The letters were from the English alphabet but they made no words that I could decipher.

"Oh, shit—here it is again," I muttered and my uncle said, "Isn't that the same signal that Poker-face left for you when you were up in the Chingbai Mountains?"

I nodded as I wondered when in hell had Qilin been in here.

"How did you find this?" I asked.

"Never mind that just now. Are you sure this is his handwriting?"

As soon as he saw my nod of assent he waved and yelled, "Hey Four-eyes. Get the others down here right away. We found the entrance."

"What the hell is going on here?" I rubbed my aching head and groaned at the thought of another mystery.

"Look at this writing and tell me the difference between this and what you saw in the mountains."

"Difference? What are you talking about?" I peered closer at the letters and noticed their color—they were dark gray, not freshly carved. This had been done quite a long time ago.

"It's impossible. How could this be so old? Let me see it again—"

Uncle Three said, "There's no reason to look any closer. It's his handwriting, he's definitely carved it, but he didn't do it just a few days ago. He carved it the last time he came to this place."

CHAPTER EIGHTEEN
THE SIGNPOST

My head pounded with pain. "I don't get it. What do you mean the last time he came? Has he been here before?"

Tracing the carved letters with his fingers, Uncle Three said, "That's right. I've seen these more than once in this place. These same letters are everywhere. I've followed them and got through the jungle in record time, reaching the camp that you found later. But I wasn't sure then whether these marks had been left by Qilin. Now that you've confirmed his handwriting, I know for certain that this isn't his first time in this place. He was here quite a long time ago."

"But that's impossible." I stammered, wanting to ask questions, but not knowing where to begin.

"Could this have happened before he lost his memory? Did he come with Wen-Jin to this place ten years ago? No, that's impossible. He lost his memory in the undersea tomb, long before Wen-Jin came here." I stopped babbling when my uncle spoke.

"I don't know for sure right now. But I've told you before that this young lad isn't that simple. Clearly his past is complex and puzzling, and he has a reason for everything he does. I'm guessing that if we follow this signal that he left here, we'll find out where he finally ended up, and we might be able to find our way out."

I felt as if my brain had frozen; thinking was beyond my grasp. I didn't know anything about Qilin's past. He might well have been here before; it was entirely possible in terms of the timeline. As I listened to Uncle Three, I noticed that he was staring at the Sunglasses Kid.

"Now what?" I asked my uncle.

He put his finger to his lips and whispered. "You're really pissing me off. You shouldn't have tagged along this time, damn it. You're a jerk who has absolutely no clue about what's going on. This time around I'm not the leader you've always known. This group of guys I pulled together at a moment's notice—I don't trust them and they don't listen to me. They could turn on me in a second—and you'd die with me. Don't you wish you'd kept out of this mess? I sure as hell wish you had."

"I had no idea. You told me..."

"Shut up!"

The Sunglasses Kid ambled toward us and Uncle Three asked, "How's everything coming along?"

"They're on their way; I told them to send the equipment down first. They asked what we should do with the fat guy. Why don't we just leave him up there and have someone to stay behind and take care of him? It's unrealistic to bring him along with us, and Young Master Wu, you don't look so good either."

"These goddamned burial cocoons are getting on my nerves," I replied. It was as convincing an excuse as any I could think up off the top of my head.

"We aren't leaving anybody behind," my uncle broke in. "Tell them to bring everything and everybody down here, and then we'll decide how to handle Fats."

"In that case, Young Master Wu, could you please lend a hand? Your pal is quite a load to carry."

I nodded and said, "I'll come once I'm done here," and the Kid walked away.

Uncle Three and I glanced at each other. Was my uncle losing his grip on reality? My impression of the Kid was favorable enough, but I was still a novice in the world of grave robbing. Truthfully the only one of the whole bunch whom I trusted was Panzi.

My uncle murmured, "Don't argue with me. I can't take care of you this time. You have to watch out for yourself. I'm so pissed off at you that when we get out, I'm going to tell your father to send you out of the country. Maybe you can make it overseas but you're too goddamned dumb to survive in our corner of the planet."

He was dead serious so I nodded meekly. In a rush of words he continued, "I'm going to keep this brief. Just remember, those guys up there are all Changsha gangsters and that kid Four-eyes is their leader. Watch out for him— and the one who calls himself Mop too. He and the guys who came with him are all fresh out of prison. Killing is like breaking an egg as far as they're concerned. Don't talk to them and don't listen to them if you want to get out of here alive."

The Kid called me, and my uncle patted me on the back. "Pay attention," he muttered.

I went back up and we managed to get Fats down to Uncle Three. I kept quiet and put on my most innocent expression as we worked. I was still unsure of my uncle's sanity or veracity but wasn't eager to put either to the test. At last we were all in the same place again. As I watched my uncle's team, they looked as though they were playing a game, wearing false faces. I was so stupefied by weariness that it was easy to play dumb and stay silent. I had little energy for anything else.

We set off in the direction of Qilin's signpost, two men carrying Fats. I clutched a double-barreled shotgun that my uncle had jammed into my hands. "For killing snakes," he told me, one eyebrow raised.

I thought about Panzi and started to feel sick. I had no idea how he was right now. The temple was probably a safer place than here, but if his fever went up again, then the odds were really against him. If he were with us, able-bodied and kicking these men into gear, Uncle Three wouldn't be such a wreck.

In less than five hundred steps, a fork appeared in the tunnel ahead of us. We searched the walls nearby and quickly found Qilin's lettering pointing us in the direction we should follow.

Uncle Three appeared excited, but now I could see that his expression was strained and fake. He waved to the team and we continued marching forward.

Moving through these shafts was boring and mind numbing, surrounded by nothing but bricks without any carvings or anything man-made. We trudged for three hours, finding and following more of Qilin's signposts on our monotonous journey. The shafts led past many reservoirs that became larger the farther we went. There was no sound, which reassured me, because I felt that meant there were no snakes. Even so, I had the persistent feeling that something invisible was lurking close by, following us.

When we finally made camp and began to rest, my nerves settled down. Several campfires illuminated our resting place and as we were eating, Fats woke up.

He had some food and then fell back to sleep, ignoring my questions of what had happened to him. But that flicker of consciousness made me feel much better; Fats was going to make it.

Sure enough, when he awoke the next morning, he was much less pallid. Although he still couldn't walk, he stood up with my help. He looked around and asked me in a feeble voice to tell him what had happened.

"Well, fat man, you have to thank me a million times. You're lucky I didn't leave you with the snakes; I risked my life to save yours. How are you going to show your gratitude to me for giving you another chance to screw up?"

Fats turned to Mop and asked meekly, "A cigarette for a wounded comrade, please?" He took a long drag and glared at me. "Fuck you. I've saved you so many times and now you're gloating over one miserable rescue? I'm telling you, we're not even yet. Where the hell are we, can you tell me that much?"

I told him briefly about everything that happened, concluding with, "Now tell me what happened to you and Qilin before the snakes carried you to me?"

"When Qilin and I were running, I couldn't keep up with him. The snakes started calling and like you, I thought they were members of your uncle's group—that they were all still alive and looking for us. But I wasn't as stupid as you were. I sneaked over as quietly as I could but when I approached, a snake got me. I'm afraid they got Qilin too—those snakes are bastards. Of course Qilin is smarter than both of us put together—maybe he's still breathing somewhere."

My uncle saw that Fats was conscious and rushed over to give him another cigarette. "Don't think that's enough, Master Three. This job is the worst I've ever been on— triple my wages or I quit here and now."

This proved that Fats was back to normal, and he recovered quickly. Within a few hours, he could walk on his own and we resumed our trek the next day. We kept going deeper. The reservoirs became larger, as did the tunnels we walked through.

We stopped at the sixth reservoir, which was half the size of a football field and was bone dry. It was too early to make camp, but roots covered with strange fungal growths obscured the openings of all the nearby tunnels. We had no idea of where to go next and we could see no helpful signs left by Qilin.

"Why are there so many roots so far underground? What tree could have such an incredible root system?"

"Those aren't roots," Mop told me. "They're mushrooms. Come on, guys. Cut them away and find the sign we're looking for."

The men searched until one of them shouted and dropped to the ground. Behind the mushrooms that he had cleared away was a face, carved into the tunnel wall. "It's moving. It smiled at me," he screamed.

I picked up a rock and the moths on the carving

fluttered away, leaving the face motionless. "My turn to laugh," I said as the terrified man regained his footing, looking humiliated.

"It's not really funny," I told him, "the moths could mean there are snakes nearby. The insects are attracted by the smell of the skins that the snakes shed." I poked around near the carving and found a huge white object shaped like a sack.

"Damn, this is all one skin. It's the size of a water bucket. And look—it has two layers of scales."

Uncle Three walked over and touched the skin; his hand came away covered in slime. "Get your rifles ready—this skin has just been shed. Hurry up and find that damned signal so we can get the hell out of here."

I joined in the search but there were no marks to be found. Damn you, Qilin—don't abandon us here, I thought as I hacked furiously at the walls of mushrooms.

There was only one place left to search and that was on the upper walls of the reservoir. We grabbed the smallest, thinnest guy in the group and made him scale the wall. He was a good climber, twisting his body and planting his feet in small niches that were almost invisible. He peered into a few tunnel openings at the very top and then shouted, "It's here."

"Get the ropes ready," Uncle Three ordered. Then a worried voice called down, "Master Three, I found another mark in another tunnel."

A streak of red flashed before our eyes and the small, thin guy came hurtling toward us, with a bloodcurdling scream. Before he hit the ground, a snake shot out of a tunnel and wrapped itself around him.

18. THE SIGNPOST

The men around me set off a volley of bullets but the snake was undeterred by the gunshots. It smashed its prey viciously against the wall several times, hurled him to his death, and then coiled down the wall. Its giant body caught several more men in its coils and sent them whirling off into midair.

In a panic some of our group raced off into the tunnels as my uncle cursed at them, yelling, "Stand and fire, you damned cowards!"

He remained in place, shooting at the reptile, and I stayed with him until the Sunglasses Kid dragged us both into a nearby tunnel. I was the last to enter and as I neared the opening I saw a large black shadow surging toward my uncle. "Watch your backs!" I screamed.

He and the Kid both turned to face a wave of snakes. We all began to fire rapidly into the crowd of reptiles, but as they died, still more oozed from the tunnels. "Too many of them," the Sunglasses Kid shouted. "We can't hope to hold out against them."

My uncle turned to me and hissed, "Run! We'll cover you while you escape—go back down the wall now—no arguing for once."

I turned and ran for my life, even though I realized there was no safety anywhere in this damned place. Then I saw that up ahead was a pile of burial cocoons. I pulled out my canteen and poured the last of my water over the dust of the closest cocoon, plastered the mud over my body, and dropped to the ground, wedging myself in between the enshrouded corpses. I held my breath and lay absolutely still.

When the snakes came, they swarmed over the cocoons

and crawled over my mud-smeared body. As they twisted their way over me, the back of my neck began to prickle—I had forgotten to smear any mud on it. One of the snakes curled over my shoulder, heading toward that clean patch of skin, and I knew I was dead.

A sound emerged from the pile of bodies. The snake stopped to see where it was coming from; as its head turned, a hand came from the burial pile and placed itself on the back of my neck. I forced myself not to scream. Slowly I looked at the cocoon closest to me. It wasn't a dead body; it was a living human covered in mud.

The snake, finding nothing in the darkness nearby, turned back to explore my bare skin, only to find that it had disappeared. It moved off, clucking to its comrades, and they all slithered away.

I remained motionless, not daring to do anything more than breathe. Only when the mysterious hand left my neck did I try to get to my feet. But my muscles had turned into jelly; it was minutes before I could finally move into a sitting position.

"Don't turn around." It was a woman's voice that I heard. Two small hands covered my eyes. "I need your shirt. Keep your eyes closed, take it off, and give it to me."

Instinctively I stretched my hands toward the voice and touched a bare shoulder. "Stop!" the woman commanded and slapped my hand away. She grabbed my shirt, and I could hear her putting it on.

"All right. You can look at me now." There in front of me was a tiny woman, so small that my shirt covered her like a bathrobe. I looked closely at her face and immediately recognized who this was. "Chen Wen-Jin. Aunt, you're here."

Wen-Jin looked at me and grinned. "You've grown up, little boy."

"And you're the same as you were in Uncle Three's photo. You look younger than I do. You haven't changed a bit in twenty years."

"You have." She laughed. "You were a lot cuter back in the days when I changed your diapers."

Suddenly I felt a strong yearning for my uncle. He had been searching for this woman for most of his life and now that I had found her, I didn't know if he was alive or dead. If he had only followed me, I thought, and struggled against tears.

"How…where…you're still so beautiful…what…so long ago." I fell silent, lost in questions, and Wen-Jin looked at me and laughed. "Not so long ago—don't you recognize me? We drank tea together at a campfire only a few days ago."

"What?" I repeated, "Tea? Where?"

Wen-Jin put her muddy hands up to her head and swept her hair into the style of a Tibetan woman. Quickly she used my shirtsleeve to wipe most of the dirt off her face and I gasped. "You're the woman who was Dingzhu-Zhuoma's daughter-in-law!"

CHAPTER NINETEEN
THE TRUTH AT LAST

"That's right. I was with you from the beginning," Wen-Jin replied, laughing at my startled face. She began to make a series of clucking sounds, which were returned to us from deep within the nearest tunnel. Is she calling the snakes, I asked myself in a quick burst of panic. Then I saw a figure coming toward us. It was Qilin.

He squeezed himself in between us, glancing at Wen-Jin and then back at me.

"What's going on?" I asked and then I knew. "Damn it. Is this a setup? You guys are partners, aren't you? Are you more than that to each other?"

Neither of them had aged over the past twenty years, both had gone on the same ill-fated archaeological expedition, at different times each of them had passed through the mysterious bronze doors. Of course they were linked; the only question was how deep was their attachment?

Qilin shook his head without saying a word. I looked at Wen-Jin and she replied, "It's not what you're thinking. There's nothing intimate between us."

"Will one of you please tell me exactly what is going on?"

"It's not complicated really," Wen-Jin explained. "Qilin recognized me when he saw me with Dingzhu-Zhuoma, but he didn't give me away. Later we found each other in this place. We haven't been working together against you; you have to believe that."

Qilin nodded as she finished speaking, and I exploded at him. "Why didn't you tell me about this? Are you working for my uncle or not? Where's your loyalty to the man who's been paying you all this time?"

"I thought you already knew," he said calmly, and Wen-Jin put her hand on my arm to keep me from lunging at his throat.

"He was right to keep silent. Otherwise, I would have fallen into the hands of that glamour girl who was leading your expedition and we wouldn't have gotten along well at all," Wen-Jin said. "Besides, at that time I didn't know which of you I could trust. I needed Qilin to check that out for me."

I suddenly remembered the night Qilin pulled at our faces to see if any of us was wearing a mask. There was the answer to one question—now on to the next five hundred.

"What about those videotapes?" I asked. "What was that all about?"

I was interrupted by a scream and a brief volley of gunshots.

Qilin grimaced at the sound. "Why don't they just send the snakes an engraved dinner invitation?"

"We have to get out of here," Wen-Jin said. "I'll tell you the whole story as soon as we're safe, I promise. Now move fast." She pointed and we raced off into the inner darkness of the tunnel.

"What's your plan?" I panted as we ran, "Don't you want to see my uncle after all these years?"

"Be quiet and listen to the water," Wen-Jin replied. "You'll notice that its noise is dying down and that means trouble. These drainage tunnels form a complicated network but when there's water flowing through them, the current provides a direction to the largest reservoir. Without water, the tunnels become a deadly maze. Luckily the rain has been heavier than usual this year, so we have more time than usual. As far as your uncle's concerned, we're all headed toward the same place. As long as he manages to stay uninjured, we'll find each other."

She glanced at her watch. "It's almost dawn. The snakes hunt aboveground at night and return to the tunnels at daybreak. We need to find a place to hide. You can ask your questions then—for now keep your mind on the road ahead."

Wen-Jin's voice was soft but commanding. This woman was a natural leader and I fell under her spell immediately. She, Qilin, and I hastened our pace and covered a lot of ground very quickly.

We entered a new tunnel and Wen-Jin ordered us to block both ends of it with rocks. "Give me your shirt," she told Qilin. She tore it to pieces and filled the gaps in our stone barricade with bits of cloth. "To the snakes, this tunnel looks closed off and impenetrable. Believe me, this is how I've stayed alive for a long, long time."

It was damp and cold in our hiding place so we built a small fire. Its light and warmth were comforting and Wen-Jin smiled at me. "Ask me whatever you like."

"There are so many questions. Can I start at the beginning of what I know?"

"Go ahead," she replied.

19. THE TRUTH AT LAST

"I want to begin with the underground tomb. After you disappeared there, where did you go? What happened to you?"

"What were you told by your uncle?"

I recounted everything Uncle Three had told me in the hospital room and Wen-Jin listened carefully, a strange smile on her face.

"Are you sure you're ready to hear the truth? I'm not sure that you'll believe me."

"You could tell me that Uncle Three is really a woman, or I'm his biological son—I'll believe you. I've been fed so many lies in the past couple of years. All I want is the truth, no matter how painful it might be."

Wen-Jin stared at Qilin for a minute, ran her fingers through the dried mud in her hair, and reached for her backpack. Pulling out a notebook, she flipped through it and handed me an old, faded photograph. I recognized it immediately. It was the group photo of the Xisha expedition before they went out to sea.

"I know this photograph very well," I said.

"This picture holds the key to all of the secrets that have tormented you. It isn't complicated but you would never see it unless you were told where to look. Now I'm going to tell you. Read the names written on the bottom of the photo and show me that person in the picture."

"I don't know all of their faces; I only recognize a few people. Here's Qilin, this is you, and here is Uncle Three."

I looked up and Wen-Jin stared into my eyes without speaking. She took the photo from my hands and asked, "Why do you think that man is your uncle?"

"This is how Uncle Three looked when he was young. I've

seen him in black-and-white photographs before. It looks just like him."

Wen-Jin smiled and said, "Resemblances don't only exist between photographs. Two people related by blood can also look very much alike."

"Wait a second. What do you mean? Are you trying to tell me that this isn't my Uncle Three? Then who is he?"

Immediately I felt little bits of ice floating through my veins and scattered puzzle pieces came together—the resemblance of those related by blood. My voice croaked as I tried to speak. "Impossible! Is the man I call Uncle Three really Jie Lianhuan?"

Wen-Jin's nod made my skin crawl and every hair on my arms stood on end. My mind knew she was telling the truth; it was my body that didn't want to accept it. I put my head between my knees, trying not to pass out.

"Which man in this picture *is* my uncle?" I whispered.

"He was the one taking the picture."

"But that can't be right. It doesn't make sense. Why did you guys make Uncle Three take the photo? Why not Jie Lianhuan, who forced himself onto your team, rather than my uncle who was a key member of the group?"

Wen-Jin took a deep breath and said, "You have a good sense of comprehension; you should be able to grasp that this is where the problem lies. Many of the things that your Uncle Three told you are fundamentally incorrect, and they all start from this beginning." She paused and then continued. "Let me tell you. In fact, the person who used his connections to join that archaeological expedition wasn't Jie Lianhuan, but your Uncle Three, Wu Sansheng."

"Huh?" I didn't know how to respond to this at all.

"Think about this carefully. Although everything seemed smooth in the story that your Uncle Three told you, everything was based on some tiny inconsistencies. As a rich and experienced smuggling tycoon, why would Jude Kao ask someone as green as Jie Lianhuan with no experience in grave robbing to carry out his plan? With the connections he had at that time, he found the most competent man for the job in Changsha, who was also a person with a strong interest in overseas smuggling—your Uncle Three. Only someone with this background, a man as bold as your Uncle Three, would cooperate with that old fox. So the person who worked with Jude Kao wasn't Jie Lianhuan but your Uncle Three. There was also another advantage to choosing Wu Sansheng, the romantic relationship between the two of us, which made it easy for him to become part of the archaeological expedition.

"Jie Lianhuan was one of the initial members of my archaeological expedition. He was a student of archaeology at the university, and because of his family connections, his father arranged for him to study in my department. This person wasn't the least bit as incompetent as the man whom you call Uncle Three has portrayed him to be. Although he had a bit of a temper, he was extremely gifted. He was reticent and an introvert, but he was meticulous in his thoughts and his grades were excellent. His one goal in life was to achieve a university degree." She paused before asking, "So now you get it, right? Your Uncle Three put everything backward."

I couldn't wrap my mind around this. Slowly I worked it out for myself: Jude Kao found Uncle Three and told him about Xisha. Uncle Three devised a plan to join the expedition team and locate the ancient tomb. Jie Lianhuan had nothing to do with any of this.

"But why did he have to reverse his role in everything? There's no reason for it, I know him very well. Are you trying to say that he deliberately told this enormous lie just to bolster his prestige? That doesn't sound like him at all."

"Why did he have to do this? Do you still not understand? He told you the opposite of the whole thing, but what happened before Xisha wasn't everything—what he's really trying to cover up is what happened afterward."

I tried to recall in detail the whole story told by Uncle Three and suddenly I felt as though I had fallen into a bottomless glacier. My blood congealed in my veins.

It wasn't Jie Lianhuan who was caught by Uncle Three when he tried to dive into the tomb that evening. It was Uncle Three who was sneaking around and was discovered by Jie Lianhuan.

Jie Lianhuan told Uncle Three to take him down to the ancient tomb, or he would tell Wen-Jin everything—so my uncle brought him to the bottom of the sea.

Everything came together. All the events began to correspond with the past records and personalities of these two men.

In the version of the story that Uncle Three told me, he had left Jie Lianhuan in the ancient tomb and had escaped by himself. But now, the most unimaginable scenario arose before me.

If everything was completely opposite from what I had been told by my uncle, the only explanation was that Jie Lianhuan was the one who came up from the ancient tomb. He had beaten Uncle Three into unconsciousness and left him to die. So the person who was now dead beneath the sea was Uncle Three and the uncle that I knew and loved… my brain froze.

Wen-Jin saw the expression on my face and said, "So you finally get it. Your so-called Uncle Three isn't Wu Sansheng, and this is why your Uncle Three will never tell you the truth. From the start, everything went wrong, and he was replaced by someone else when they were both under the sea."

"But, but how is this possible? Why didn't his brothers know an imposter had taken my uncle's place?"

"Your Uncle Three was always eccentric. He was aloof and lived on his own from the time he was in his teens. For years he barely ever saw his family. All Jie Lianhuan needed was a little makeup and a little knowledge of your Uncle Three's character in order to deceive everyone. I think you also know in your deepest heart that the Uncle Three you know today is completely different from the Uncle Three in your earliest childhood memories."

My clothes were soaked with the sweat that had broken out all over my body. A man who had been gone for five or six years, who suddenly reappeared with a rather different temperament and a slightly changed appearance, would be accepted by a family who hadn't been close to him for a long time. And my "uncle's" changes had all been for the better. When he was young, he was a lawless savage. After the disappearance of the woman he loved, he had become quieter and more thoughtful.

"But, Uncle…Jie Lianhuan—why did he have to do this? Why did he have to swap identities with my Uncle Three?"

"This is an extremely complex situation. He might have

done it for the official records. After he came back from the ancient tomb, all of us were gone. If Jie Lianhuan had stayed with the unit as he should have, that he was the only one not to disappear would pose a pretty serious problem for him. On the other hand, Wu Sansheng wasn't officially part of the expedition. His name wasn't in any of the files, so nobody would know that he was connected to this matter. He was in the clear. So after the Jie family weighed all the pros and cons, they might have decided to go along with this change of identity. At the same time, Jie Lianhuan would also of course take possession of Wu Sansheng's business; that would be beneficial for the Jie family, whose fortunes were gradually declining. However, once this lie was told, it could never end.

"You know your Uncle Two was notorious in Changsha for being a person who should never be provoked. If he knew that his younger brother had been killed and his identity usurped by his murderer, he would have ruthlessly come after the Jie family. And with the power structure of your grandfather's family, this scandal would inevitably stir up a foul wind and a rain of blood," Wen-Jin said. "I've been discreetly following this matter; I tried to communicate the real story to your family in some way, but Jie Lianhuan frightened me. This man is extremely thorough, and I had a feeling that if I just popped out one day and divulged the whole cover-up, he would somehow shift the blame onto me. The only thing I could do was hide."

I covered my face, feeling a surge of disbelief. This couldn't possibly be true. I said, "In that case, what happened to you in Xisha? Why did you guys suddenly disappear? And why were there words written in blood on the ceiling of the ancient tomb that said Wu Sansheng harmed me? If Jie Lianhuan truly killed Uncle Three, then the words should have said the exact opposite. No, this doesn't make sense at all. You're lying to me too, along with everyone else who was part of your damned expedition."

Wen-Jin looked at me with the expression of someone who was suffering a terrible headache. "Young Wu. You've known this man for so many years. I know you can't possibly believe this, so I considered not telling you at all. But you're too tied up in this mystery; even if I didn't tell you now, I don't think that man could keep lying to you for much longer. There are too many holes in his story. Unless he continued to feed you with lies, he would have no choice but to come out with the truth. And you know very well, it's too late for you to choose to disbelieve what I've just told you."

I struggled to calm myself before managing to choke out, "I know. Please go on. I'm just letting off some steam. This is hard for me to hear."

Wen-Jin put my hand in her tiny palm and lightly patted it with her other hand. I stopped shuddering and she continued, "You may find the things that follow even harder to believe."

Uncle Three's death from drowning was an unexpected accident. When his body was found, clutching the Bronze Fish with Snake Brows in one hand, his ulterior motives clearly suspicious, Wen-Jin was heartbroken and sick with grief. But the situation that cropped up immediately afterward kept her from mourning. She had no choice but to continue with the expedition, and she led the team down to the undersea tomb.

What happened hereafter basically corresponded with what "Uncle Three," or Jie Lianhuan, told me. He was probably afraid that the real Uncle Three had left behind a clue or two that would link him to what had happened in the ancient tomb, so he pretended to be sick. After the others had begun their exploration, he secretly followed them and in the end, he truly was separated from the group.

As far as he knew, Wen-Jin and the others had disappeared in the tomb and would never be seen again. That was when he got the idea of posing as Uncle Three and stealing his identity. When he was rescued, he told the fisherman who came to his aid that he was Wu Sansheng. If he hadn't done that, he would have been unmasked at the very start. All this was very well thought out; Wen-Jin's description of Jie Lianhuan as a deliberate and focused person was unquestionably accurate.

But what had happened to Wen-Jin and the others after they had walked deep into the tomb? Up to now all I knew was that they finally reached the hall where the model of the Cloud-Top Temple was placed and then were drugged by someone who looked a lot like Uncle Three.

Wen-Jin said, "You're not going to want to hear this and you certainly won't want to believe it." She looked at me questioningly.

"No need to worry about my feelings at this stage of the game."

"The person who drugged us wasn't someone who looked like your Uncle Three. It was your Uncle Three."

An Uncle Three here and an Uncle Three there—I was becoming a little confused about which Uncle Three was real and which was fake. "Let's just use their real names. Do you mean that the person who drugged you guys was really Wu Sansheng? But hadn't his body already come to the surface and been identified?"

"We made a mistake. The body that we recovered at sea wasn't Wu Sansheng. It was probably someone from the team that Jude Kao had hired before he found your uncle. The corpse's face had been smashed against the rocks to the point that it was no longer recognizable and its body was swollen beyond recognition. We identified him as Wu Sansheng because he wore the same diving suit that Jude Kao had given to all of us. I had felt doubtful that this was the man I loved, but I'm no forensic expert and he was wearing the same suit that Wu Sansheng used."

"Well then, according to what Qilin told me, my uncle was preening like a woman when you first saw him and then he tried to escape into the tunnel behind the mirror. Then he drugged you all. Why did he do that?"

"Because he thought that Jie Lianhuan had already told me everything," Wen-Jin explained. "He thought I had come down to denounce him publicly. It would have been better if I had come alone, but since the entire archaeological team had come with me, he assumed that his scheme had been exposed, which was a very serious crime. As the leader of the expedition, I couldn't possibly let him go unpunished in front of so many people. He had to protect himself, and to a degree me too, so he decided to drug us before deciding what to do next."

"So that was the last scene," I said. "That makes sense, but what about the words written in blood?"

"Those words are a problem you made yourself. You misread the sentence," Wen-Jin said. "Think about it. How were the words arranged?"

How could I possibly have misread it? To get to the bottom of this, I dipped my finger in the water kettle and wrote the words on the wall as I remembered them.

Wu	harmed	Jie
Sansheng	me	Lianhuan

Instantly I realized what my mistake had been. "My God. I read it the wrong way!"

I had been in the antique business for too long. Everything on ancient stone rubbings is read in the opposite order, so I always read from the opposite direction when sentences were written in a vertical alignment. I was used to reading from left to right, but this sentence could be read either way, with opposite meanings depending upon how they were read.

"So you have no doubts now, right?" Wen Jin asked.

Embarrassed, I nodded and asked, "Then what happened?"

Her expression changed as she continued, "I still don't understand the things that happened afterward because we were no longer in the undersea tomb when we woke up. Instead, we were in a basement, a very old basement like one of those caves built in the sixties, with a black sarcophagus in the middle. We found the exit of the basement, but it was closed off, and we couldn't open it no matter how hard we tried. From the date on my watch, I knew we had been in a coma for over a week."

"And that was the nursing home in Golmud?" I asked.

She nodded and paused before continuing. "A few of us were missing, Qilin was gone, and some other people whom we didn't know were being held in the same place. Then we found out that we were being watched."

CHAPTER TWENTY
IMPRISONMENT

After Wen-Jin had been drugged by Uncle Three, her memory went blank. When they woke up, they were already inside the nursing home in Golmud. Obviously they had been kidnapped and locked in that place while they were still unconscious.

"Wu Sansheng wasn't with you guys?"

Wen-Jin shook her head. Then I asked, "That's strange. Then who kidnapped you?"

"It's '*It*.'" She replied in an almost deathlike tone of voice.

"What is '*It*'?"

Wen-Jin took a sip of water and slowly shook her head as she explained, "I can't describe *It*. *It* is what we discovered as we ventured further into the unknown. How can I describe this to you…think of a kind of powerful force.

"After we survived, we made a lot of speculations about our experience from beginning to end, during the time we spent in that dark house. However, we couldn't connect many aspects of what had happened, and finally we realized that one of us was always missing at many locations where the events took place." Wen-Jin brushed her hair behind her ears. "But a few people couldn't have caused all these things to happen. Still, they did happen, and it seemed as though there was an invisible being pulling the strings. The more we studied the whole thing, the more certain we were that this entity definitely exists, but up until now, *It* hasn't given *Itself* away. *It* seems to be a shapeless intangible abstraction—as if *It* only exists in logic.

"We began to call this 'It.' There's Jude Kao, Jie Lianhuan, and us—and then there's a force that's intervening in this whole thing, and this force is deeply hidden. *It* almost never shows its face. But its strength drives the development of everything that's happened to us, and *It* terrifies me."

Her words made me shudder again. "Can you give me an example?"

"Was the silk book really decoded by Jude Kao? How could a foreigner solve such a complex puzzle? Besides, how did he become aware of the existence of the undersea tomb? If no one had told him, then he wouldn't have come to China; he wouldn't have bought the services of your Uncle Three, and he wouldn't still be clinging to a goal which nobody else knows anything about. Also—"

Wen-Jin sat up, squared her shoulders, and swept up her hair again, showing her oval face. "Every one of us seems to have lost the ability to age. So many years have passed and we have grown no older." Her posture was elegant and she looked so beautiful that I almost stopped breathing. But she immediately let her hair fall back down again, shook it out, and said, "After we fell unconscious, someone must have done something to our bodies."

20. IMPRISONMENT

"Staying young is a good thing," I said. "Many people dream of this happening to them."

Wen-Jin shook her head and said, "Dream? Do you still remember the thing that you ran into down in the basement in Golmud?"

"How could I forget?"

"That will be how we all will look in the end," Wen-Jin said. "The thing you saw was Huo Ling."

"What? That monster was Huo Ling?" Instantly I felt so nauseated that I almost fell to my knees.

"After she returned from Tamu-Tuo, she began to change," Wen-Jin said, "and then she turned into a monster."

"That…"

"There are side effects to this seemingly permanent youth." She looked at me, held out her hand, and said, "Smell my skin." I sniffed and a very familiar aroma flowed through my nostrils. It was the scent of the Forbidden Lady.

"At a certain time, we will begin to transform. These changes have already begun to take place in my body. Very soon, I will become exactly like the monster that you saw."

CHAPTER TWENTY-ONE

THE RENDEZVOUS

I stared at Wen-Jin, feeling that everything she had told me had turned to fantasy with this last disclosure.

"So *It* did something to you, making you unable to grow old, but that would eventually turn you into that kind of... monster?"

Wen-Jin nodded. "From what I've seen, it takes only about six months for a body to deteriorate into what Huo Ling became. We watched her slowly transform, which was both horrible and terrifying. It was as though her body bypassed death and changed directly from a living person into a moving corpse."

"But how is this possible? Is there an antidote?"

"No. The time that it takes to transform into a corpse varies from one individual to another. The only sign that it has begun is the odor that the victim's skin gives off. Our first theory was that we had been infected somehow with this process when we were unconscious in the undersea tomb, that perhaps it was an ancient virus that had been preserved in the subterranean tunnels, waiting for its next victims. Later we discovered this wasn't the case, but that it was somehow connected to Wang Canghai."

"And that's why you began to do research on him?"

"Yes," she replied, "but there's more to the Golmud story that you need to hear. We were trapped in the basement of the old house for a long time before we found our way out. Then we realized we were being hunted in the city. It was unfamiliar territory for us so we decided to double back and take refuge in the nursing home, thinking nobody would suspect that we'd return to the place we had struggled to escape. Then Huo Ling began to change…"

"So you believe there's no cure in the world that might stop this?"

"We found that Wang Canghai was trying hard to find a secret of immortality that had been recorded in the silk book of the Warring States period, but apparently it wasn't a fully developed process and we might have become guinea pigs. Although we could remain youthful, eventually the process broke down and turned young bodies into monsters. The recorded text in the Warring States silk book came from this place, so I thought we might find some written information that could help us here. But it was too late for Huo Ling. She started to become forgetful and she lost control of her emotions. Her metabolism sped up, and finally she turned into that unrecognizable creature. About a month ago, I began to smell that odor on my own skin and I knew what my fate would be. But first I have to tie up the loose ends that dangle in this story and do my best to explain it to you."

"But what does any of this have to do with me? Why did you send me the videotapes?"

"I wasn't the one who sent you the tapes," Wen-Jin said. "That's another unexplained mystery. When I saw you were part of Ning's team, I was shocked, so I told

Dingzhu-Zhuoma to have you brought to our tent. Because you were in the group, I could tell that *It* had infiltrated the expedition somehow; *It* sent you the videotapes that I had originally sent to Jude Kao."

"Why?"

"I'm not sure. But I know *It* is trying to find me."

I rubbed my eyes hard, feeling a bit more clear. "How long do you have left before your transformation takes place? Do we have time to find a way to save you?"

She took my hand again and said, "Don't worry about me. I accept all the arrangements my fate has in store for me, good or bad. This is my destiny, and Qilin's, as well as Jie Lianhuan's. You have to think about saving yourself."

I looked at Qilin and Wen-Jin, thinking it was pointless to believe I'd get out of this place if neither one of them was planning to. At that moment, we heard someone gently knocking on the barrier of stones that we had put at the entrance. A voice asked, "Is there anybody in here?"

Qilin nodded reassuringly and moved some rocks aside. There was Fats, along with several men, including the Sunglasses Kid.

Fats's mud-covered face split into a broad grin when he saw me. "So you're safe, young comrade, and you've found your mystery woman. How did this happen?"

"Too long a story to tell now, Fats. How did you find us? Where's my uncle?"

"He's not too far behind us. He was bitten by a snake and had to stop to be treated with serum. We found a crevice, came inside, and heard voices. I was almost afraid to find out who was talking. I thought it was those damned snakes again," Fats replied with a sigh.

Although I knew that the man I called my uncle was really Jie Lianhuan, I couldn't stop caring about him. I turned to Wen-Jin, wondering if she would let me go in search of "Uncle Three." She looked into my eyes, smiled, and said, "Go and find him. I'll come with you."

We found the rest of the group not too far away, all of them pale and exhausted. Mop took us to Uncle Three, who looked like hell, with bloody punctures on his neck and shoulders. He looked at me with clouded eyes and mumbled something incoherent.

"The snake killed three of our people before it bit him. Its venom was almost depleted by that time, but it was still poisonous," Mop said.

Uncle Three opened his eyes slightly. I didn't see him look at Wen-Jin, but he probably did. I saw him shiver a little, then he looked at me, as though he was unsure of what to say.

My heart ached. Watching his face, I simply couldn't imagine that he wasn't really my uncle. I had always loved him, enjoyed his company, and hung out with him after I grew up. Even if he was Jie Lianhuan, all of my memories and impressions of Uncle Three came from this man. That was unchangeable, even with what I knew now.

Wen-Jin walked over and sat down beside him. She looked at him without saying a word, and the two remained still for a while. Then Uncle Three suddenly struggled to reach out to her.

Wen-Jin took his hand and said softly, "Young Wu knows. You don't have to keep hiding the truth. We don't blame you."

He moved his lips as tears streamed down his face. He

glanced at me, then at Wen-Jin, using every ounce of his strength to try to speak.

Wen-Jin leaned down to his lips and listened to what he said. Then she held his hand even tighter. "I know. It's not your fault."

He looked at me and I held his other hand. I didn't know what I was supposed to say. Everything had happened so fast. Yesterday we were still comrades, but now he was lying here as though he was about to die. The words just slipped out. "Uncle Three."

When he heard me call him Uncle Three, he suddenly became agitated, thrashed about for a minute, and then slowly lost consciousness. I thought he was dying and immediately cried out for help. Mop came over, checked him quickly, and said, "Don't worry. He just fainted."

I took a deep breath and heard someone shout, "Look! There's a stone door here."

We all walked over and found that three men had discovered a slab of stone at the bottom of the reservoir with two iron loops attached to it. Pulling on the loops, they lifted away the slab. Beneath it was a deep hole.

Qilin and the Sunglasses Kid plunged down to investigate and returned quickly. "It's a whole other world down there," the Kid burst out. "It's a huge cave surrounded by other stone doors. The air is fresh and we didn't see a trace of snakes. Let's go and see where we can go from there. We need to find another way out of this place, unless we want to face the snakes again."

"Let's not rush into anything without checking it carefully," I warned. "Qilin and the Kid, lead the way. Fats, Wen-Jin, and I will follow. The rest of you stay with

Master Three and wait for us to return with a report on conditions down there."

We found ourselves in a huge, ring-shaped cavern with stone doors on every wall. As we peered about, I saw that Mop, instead of waiting for us above, was on the ground with us, tearing into a bag of equipment.

"Why are you here? You were told to stay with Master Three."

"He has enough nursemaids. I'm more useful down here—and so are they." He beckoned toward more of his team that was climbing down to join us, eyes glowing with greed. The man I called my uncle was right; these men weren't to be trusted.

Wen-Jin whispered to me, "Leave them alone. They're renegades, with allegiance to no man. They want treasure and they're all armed. We can do nothing; let them take what they want."

She was right. Master Three was out of commission and I had no authority over these thugs. Everything was out of control now and whatever goal we might have could be shot to hell by these mutineers.

Fats tightened his grip on his shotgun and looked at me. I shook my head. The odds were all wrong for any sort of confrontation. "Follow Qilin, just as we had planned," I told him.

We began to grope our way down a long corridor where a staircase spiraled down into a man-made cave. It was too dark for our flashlights, so Fats lit a low-level flare, designed for handheld illumination. It revealed a high-ceilinged cavern, its walls packed solid with black statues, all of them with bloated bodies. The walls were carved into graduated steps, like the seats of a stadium, and each step was crammed tight with these statues.

I suddenly remembered the mezzanine in the palace of doom where corpses filled recesses in the walls. Could these statues be mummified bodies? As the flare burned lower, we saw a stone disc on the floor, surrounded by a dozen pieces of bronze vessels, all of different shapes and sizes. That was all there was. We were at the end of our trail.

"This cave is so damned deep. Why did they dig so far below the queen's city?" Fats asked.

"This might be the holy site of her empire, where the royal family of the Queen of the West conducted their secret rituals," Wen-Jin replied.

"Pretty shabby for royalty. Look at that bronze work—primitive—and those miserable statues—oh, holy shit... Young Wu, look at what those are carved from."

I grabbed his flare and looked closely at the statues; each one of them was a figure carved from deep green jade.

"Hell. Remember the jade figures in the cavern of the blood zombies? What disaster are we in for here?"

Qilin said nothing but his face furrowed into a worried frown.

"Do you suppose each of these holds a living corpse?" Fats began to chatter as he climbed onto one of the steps where the statues rested.

"Wait, damn you," I said as I pulled him back. "Let's get to the bottom of the stairs before we begin to explore anything."

We continued down the stone staircase. At the bottom, Fats climbed up to one of the jade statues and peered at it under the beam of his flashlight. "There's a corpse in there all right, a dried-up mummy. It looks as though each statue holds one, as far as I can see," he told us.

"It looks like our Big Sister is right. This really might be where they came to perform special rituals and ceremonies," he continued. "But damn it. Could these dry bones here be the Assembly of Immortals, who gathered together underneath the kingdom of the Queen of the West as it's been described in mythology? This looks nothing like the stories."

"But these jade figures are a bit different from the ones at the cavern of the blood zombies," I said. "The bodies there were alive. These seem to be desiccated mummies."

"That's because of time. This cave was probably excavated during a period of great prosperity of the queen's empire. That would be five thousand years ago. Having gone through so many centuries, anything that held water would become air-dried."

Fats stretched out his hand to touch the black shell of the jade figurine but Qilin grabbed him. "Don't touch anything."

"Come here," Wen-Jin called to us. She was looking at the bronze vessels and when I joined her, I was amazed at their size. Every one of them was larger than I was, and each had a different shape.

"What do you suppose they were used for?" I asked and Wen-Jin muttered, "Oh my God, this is the Alchemy Chamber of the Queen of the West. It wasn't just a legend; it really exists."

She was standing beside a huge slab of stone in the center of the floor. We all gathered around to look at it; it was an astrolabe made of stone, with small dots like a star map scattered all over it. Each small dot was made from a tiny, dark green, malformed pebble.

They were the pills of immortality that Uncle Three had shown me when he was still in the hospital—but here there were so many of them.

"What's this? Is it the elixir?" A voice came from behind. It was Mop with some of his henchmen.

I quickly shook my head and said, "This is poison that would cause immediate death. You can't touch these pills of immortality. They're extremely toxic."

"Of course I'm not going to touch them. Can't I just take a look?"

"No," I said. "You can't come close to these things. They're far too dangerous. You'll risk all of our lives with one false move."

Mop lit a cigarette and raised one eyebrow. "Who do you think you are, coming up with these rules?" His attitude had lost all the deference it had carried when I first met him.

"Send up another flare, Fats. Let's get a better look at this place without endangering anyone," I said, ignoring the group nearby.

"Hell, let's make it two," Fats agreed and then let out a yelp as the first flare burst into flame. At the very top of the cave hung an interwoven network of chains, running from the wall to a giant black orb that loomed above us.

"What the hell is that?" Mop yelped.

"It's a floating furnace," Wen-Jin gasped. "Unbelievable. It's the highest realm of alchemy. The furnace doesn't touch the ground; it collects the essence of everything around it."

"Let's get a better look." Fats launched a larger flare that struck the edge of the huge black ball. The flame revealed a spherical bronze pot surrounded by chains, its size more than three times larger than any of the huge bronze vessels on the cavern floor. From where we stood, it looked like a mammoth tarantula resting in the center of a spiderweb.

"No more flares," Wen-Jin said. "Who knows what flammable substance is in that furnace. It could blow us to fragments as thoroughly as any antiballistic missile."

Then she whirled around and yelled, "What the hell are you guys doing?"

We turned to see Mop and two of his gang approaching the pills of immortality that were embedded in the astrolabe. "Don't worry, pretty little comrade. I know what I'm doing, more than the old fool who thought he was in charge of this expedition. Grab her, one of you idiots."

"Let her go, damn you," I shouted, but another of Mop's men immediately pulled out a pistol and aimed it at my head. Fats rushed over, shotgun raised, but the guy with the pistol barked, "Drop it, Fatso, or this guy is dead meat." Cursing, Fats threw his rifle to the ground.

Mop laughed. "Young Master Three, do you really think you're our master? Times have changed. Nobody cares about your lineage anymore—to hell with your grandfather and your useless uncle too."

Prying out a pill of immortality, he shone his flashlight upon it. Qilin lunged toward him, shouting, "You've changed everything—now we'll all pay for it!"

The astrolabe shook as though an earthquake had struck it. A thunderous crash came from the jade statues. Each of them lost their jade coverings and as those shrouds hit the ground, the shapes within stood before us, ancient corpses with horrible horse faces.

From the cave's opening came the sound of a closing door and the click of a lock. We were trapped in a cave full of mummies that were changing more rapidly than any of us had bargained for.

All of us stood paralyzed as the sounds of clicking began to fill the air. The dried flesh of the mummies began to flake away, as if they were coming back to life, and what emerged was the bright red skin of blood zombies.

"Do something! You're the experts," Mop screamed.

Fats snorted as he picked up his rifle. "You thought you were in charge just a minute ago and look where that got us. Let's see who can live the longest now."

He took careful aim and fired at one of the zombies. There was no wound, only a tiny puncture with no blood.

He set off another volley of shots, rapidly followed by gunfire from Mop and his men.

"That's right—join forces," Fats yelled. "We'll probably all die, but not without a fight."

Tossing me the flare gun, he shouted, "Don't shoot high—fire at their faces."

"High?" I suddenly remembered my grandfather's narrative at the beginning of his notebooks—blood zombies, he said, couldn't climb trees. If that was the case, then they wouldn't be able to scale a wall either.

"We have to find a way to climb up to the chains," I shouted. "Whoever built that furnace had to have made a way to get up to it. We have to climb away from these damned things before they kill us—it's our only hope."

"Men with guns, cover the men without weapons," Fats ordered, "the rest of you find a way up and out of here."

I rushed to the side of one of the giant bronze vessels, thinking I could climb to the top and get a better look. Once I reached the top, I realized that was high enough to get us out of harm's way. "Climb up here," I yelled and everyone scrambled to the top of the nearest mountain of bronze.

"This won't work," Fats cried out. "Not high enough! But look at this." He pulled a clump of grenades from his waistband. "I'll run toward them and clear a path with these. You guys cover me from behind and we'll head straight through these bastards."

"Where the hell did you get those?" I yelled.

"Didn't I say last time that I'd never go grave robbing again without explosives?" Fats called out. "You should pay attention to what I say, Young Wu. I only have four grenades and we have a lot of ground to cover so run like hell, everyone."

He pulled hard and the detonator shot out into the group of zombies. There was a thundering explosion and zombies flew into the air; we ducked and covered our heads to guard against cascading debris and body parts. When the dust cleared, I saw a hole had been blasted into the wall in front of us.

Fats launched a second grenade and shouted, "Run!"

We immediately leaped from the bronze furnace, just as the second explosion hit. Gravel rained down upon our heads like bullets, but we raced toward the gate without thinking of anything else. Fats threw another grenade and every man with a rifle opened fire upon the zombies that still raced toward us.

Fats yelled out, "It's the last one, guys. Let's get out of here!" He threw the last grenade toward the gate and we knew this blast was our last hope of survival.

But nothing happened, no noise, no explosion.

"Shit," Fats groaned. "It's a dud."

The zombies were closing in fast and the air reeked of blood and gunpowder.

"Quick, Fats!" I yelled. "Fire at the detonator."

"I can't see it," Fats gasped. "Too many corpses in the way."

Out of nowhere Qilin leaped onto Fats's shoulders, then propelled himself into the air, his knees landing on the back of a zombie. Twisting its head, he broke its neck like a breadstick, then stepped on it and pushed the corpses away from the grenade. Fats dashed forward and opened fire; the detonator exploded immediately.

We were much too close to the explosion, and its force blew us about like rag dolls in a tornado. I crawled onto my knees and shook my head to clear my vision. The gate was still intact. "Damn it," I heard Fats shout. "This thing is solid bronze. We're dead."

It's all over. I got to my feet, saw the zombies pooling around us, and knew we were completely done for this time. Before I steadied myself, another loud boom came from behind me, shaking the entire cave and throwing us to the ground once more. As soon as I was able to see, I turned around and discovered that the chains suspending the hanging furnace had broken from the vibration of the explosion. The furnace had sunk deep into the floor of the cave, its enormous weight making a huge crater.

The zombies were undeterred by this disturbance and circled around us, coming in for the kill. We backed up to the furnace in full retreat as Qilin yelled to Fats, "Throw me your knife!"

Fats took out his dagger and threw it over to Qilin, who caught it in midair and swiftly drew it across the palm of his hand, turning the wound toward the zombies. Attracted by the smell of blood, they turned their attention toward him, following him as he moved away from the rest of us.

We took advantage of this and rushed back to the hole created by the fall of the bronze furnace. "What are you doing?" I shouted at Qilin. He ignored me, and Fats pulled me along, forcing me to keep moving. We continued to run as Qilin was swallowed up in an ocean of zombies, leaving not even a trace of his shadow.

"Holy shit," Mop breathed as he ran. "What a sacrifice to the cause."

I grabbed the gun in his hand and shouted, "Sacrifice, my ass!" I turned to rush back into the maelstrom of zombies, to live or die with Qilin, but Fats grabbed me again and slapped me hard. "Get in there, damn you. He can take care of himself. Look!"

There was Qilin, rising out of the mob of killers, climbing up the walls of the cave, then leaping to the edge of the crowd. He ducked down almost parallel to the ground, rapidly dashed thorough the remaining zombies, and came panting to where we stood.

"Stop staring like idiots," he barked as he approached. "Find an escape route before they get to us."

Deep cracks and crevices had appeared beside the

sunken furnace and we could see more spaces beneath the cave in which we stood. Quickly we scrambled down along the side of the furnace, following the path made by a large crack in the ground.

At the bottom was a space so small that we had to get down on our hands and knees to enter it. Quickly we covered our entry point with large rocks until there was no gap to be seen. Then we all collapsed onto the floor of the small cave, trying to breathe normally again. Wen-Jin tore the sleeve of her shirt to make a bandage for Qilin's bleeding hand, and Fats looked about with his flashlight.

"It's a small man-made chamber," he observed. "No room to stretch out here—but at least we're safe for now. Wait! What the hell is this?"

We peered into the area that his flashlight illuminated and saw something carved into the rock, a sentence written in Qilin's script.

"Does this mean there's a way out of here?" Fats asked, turning toward Qilin.

Crawling over to the inscription, Qilin examined it silently and then shook his head without a word. He touched the carving with his abnormally long, sensitive fingers, then picked up a rock and began to pound upon the wall. In a few minutes, he uncovered a narrow tunnel, just wide enough for one body at a time.

"Will somebody tell me why would there be a grave robber's tunnel here?" Fats demanded.

"It's not a grave robber's tunnel. It's a channel," Qilin answered as he started making his way in.

We all looked at one another and followed him in single file. After crawling about thirty feet, we made a steep descent and as we walked downward, we heard the sound of water.

That meant that this channel was connected to an irrigation canal. Immediately we accelerated our speed, soon reaching the end, but found our path blocked by a small boulder. Qilin hurled his body against it several times and it rolled away, leaving an opening in a wall of rock. The water noises grew louder and more distinct.

Sticking our heads from the opening, we saw a wide stream outside. The current was gentle and the water looked as if it was no higher than a man's waist. It was clear; we could see the flat stones that it flowed over.

Qilin led us all into the water, Fats sweeping the area with his flashlight. Upstream was an iron gate, below us at the other end was total darkness. We approached the gate and shook it. It was immovable.

"What is this place?" Mop asked.

"It might lead to the main channel at the very bottom of the reservoir," Wen-Jin said. Her voice had hardly faded when someone yelled. We turned around and saw a statue of a human-faced bird about six and a half feet tall, standing in the middle of the stream, not too far away. We walked over and saw that the statue looked almost exactly the same as the one we had seen earlier in the rainforest.

As I began to examine it, I heard Qilin gasp softly. He moved around the statue and began walking downstream. Without asking any questions, we all followed.

21. THE RENDEZVOUS

CHAPTER TWENTY-TWO
COMING TO THE END

The stream became wider and the ceiling above grew higher and higher. A horn-shaped opening emerged and I quickened my pace. Soon the ceiling darkened and we were out of the channel. The space around us echoed as we entered it; I could tell that we had come to a huge place. A shoal extended under our feet, and the rays of Fats's flashlight revealed a broad, calm pool of water stretching before us.

Gradually we were able to see that we were in a huge underground volcanic cave filled with water. In the distance, a large number of giant pillars hung from the ceiling into the bottom of the pool, looking like the majestic pillars of a temple.

On both sides of the waterway were gigantic cliffs with the unique characteristics of volcanic rocks. We had clearly come deep into the underground mountain range of the Gobi Desert. These cliffs had to be part of the Kunlun mountain range.

I turned to look at the waterway opening and had a feeling that it had been excavated by men. That a place of this depth could be dug in the era of the Queen of the West was a clear sign that this civilization possessed extremely well developed engineering skills.

This underground lake was probably the apex of the underground reservoir system of the Queen of the West's empire. It was impossible to see how large this lake was, or how deep the center might be. After we observed the area for a while, Fats blurted out, "Now what the hell should we do?"

"We need to find another one of Qilin's signposts. The last one pointed the way to this place, and the road ahead has to be at the center of this lake," I said. "The mark we're looking for couldn't have been engraved underwater; I have a hunch we'll find it on one of these pillars."

We broke apart into groups for the search, wading through the water toward the deepest part of the lake while shining our lamps on the pillars.

After only a few steps, I found that the lake wasn't deep at all. Occasionally there were spots where we were submerged up to our necks, but after a few steps we would rise out of the water again. Clearly there were many potholes at the bottom, but on average the changes in depth weren't significant. Soon the Sunglasses Kid whistled and called us over. There was a sign engraved on one of the pillars.

Wen-Jin looked at Qilin and said, "The water current here is almost still and doesn't seem to be flowing forward. I think we're at the lowest point of the entire water reservoir project. The place we're looking for must be ahead. We're almost there. Can't you remember anything?"

He shook his head, silently staring at the sign he had

carved, without a trace of emotion in his eyes.

"Legend says the ancient city of the Queen of the West was located in a secret place, surrounded by lakes and an oasis." Fats said. "Fog covered the oasis year-round and the kingdom could only be seen during heavy rain. The underground water storage system beneath the ancient city was as intricate and complex as any maze. We've now almost exhausted all of our resources to reach the lowest level of this defense line project. If the Queen of the West was hiding anything, it would have to be here. There's no need to say another word. All we have to do is follow the sign and reach our goal."

I kept feeling that something was off-kilter. This last part of our journey had gone too smoothly, and I couldn't dismiss the menace held by the statues of birds with human faces that we had seen along the way. We knew full well that these figures were warning signs left by the Empire of the Queen of the West. When we had entered the canyon at the outset of this expedition, each time we saw one of these statues, we had encountered another danger. Finding one now clearly indicated that this reservoir wasn't a place without perils. Exhausted as we all were, I doubted we could make our way safely through another disaster, if we were unlucky enough to encounter one.

"What's our next strategy?" I asked Wen-Jin. "Should we take a break or send someone to explore the path?"

Wen-Jin replied, "We're already here. Just as Fats said, there's no reason for me to back down or give up. This is my destiny, but there's no need for all of you to go with me. You guys take a break; I'll be okay on my own. If I don't come back after two hours, you look for another exit along the lakeshore and find a way to get out. No matter what, don't come looking for me."

Qilin muttered, "I'm going too."

"So am I," I said. "Didn't I go through all the hardships on this journey just for this moment? Besides, the fact that I made it this far with my puny strength only happened because other people sacrificed themselves for me—look at Panzi, half-dead and alone, and Ning who died long before she should have. If I'm just going to cower in this place like a wimp, then I shouldn't have come in the first place. Since I made the decision to come, I'm going through with this to the bitter end."

Fats grinned. "Well, hell—aren't you just forcing me to come with you? It'd be safer to stick with you guys than hang around with these rookies."

"We have to go too," Mop insisted. "If at least one of you won't stay here with us, we'll all go. You're not leaving us to die in this godforsaken place."

The Sunglasses Kid didn't say a word; he stood watching us with his usual smile, then walked over and put his hand on my shoulder. Obviously he was coming too—or maybe he was suggesting I stay behind.

Fats said, "Young Wu. Forget about it. You still have some good years left. Stay with these men, and you might still find a way out. Didn't your Uncle Three say that we're on a road with no return? Let me take this trip with our Big Sister and our poker-faced friend. At least you'll survive to burn some incense at my grave."

"Damn you, Fats. Don't sweet-talk me. We're all in this together and I'm just as likely to die here as I will be with you."

That was the truth. Who had the confidence to say that he would definitely make it out of here alive? Who was to say that the way we came in would be our way out? We were underground, in a completely closed cave. It was almost inevitable that we would starve to death here.

I patted Fats on the back. "But look at you. If something happened to you, your mistresses back at home might rip off each other's heads trying to rob the treasure you have stashed away. It makes more sense for you to stay."

"So here we are. Not only do I have to die with you, I also have to take care of you. This thing between us—it's called fate. If you go, I'll be there to protect you. The rest of you jerks, give me your ammunition. I'm the only one here who can make a bullet count," Fats blustered.

"Enough nonsense," Wen-Jin interrupted. "If we're all going, then let's stop wasting time."

To nobody's surprise, Mop pulled out a hip flask filled with whiskey. To everyone's surprise, he passed it around and we all took a few swigs, even Wen-Jin. Then we waded across the pool in the direction of Qilin's signpost. Wen-Jin divided us into groups, each responsible for watching their section of the pool for suspicious ripples. But the only disturbance in the water was our own movements, and the water was so clear that we could easily have seen anything that might be in it. There was nothing visible at all, but still I felt uneasy.

Wen-Jin read my mind. "Corpse-eating insects aren't found in this place. Don't worry, Young Wu."

Fats nodded. "It might be because of the water temperature. Come to think of it, it's pretty damned cold. It could be that a lot of the water here was caught when this cave was formed. It's passed a shelf life of probably more than ten thousand years. Don't anybody drink it; it will probably cause diarrhea, and that's all we really need."

"If this is old water, it's probably loaded with natural minerals," I said. "Maybe some of them are toxic and that prevents the insects from swimming to this spot. But they could be somewhere in the darkness, on the rocks."

Fats groaned. "No way, really? No wonder my ass is itching. Do any of the rest of you feel anything weird?"

No one responded, but Qilin shot us a glance that shut us all up and we continued into the depths of the reservoir. Our flashlights shone across the calm waters without revealing any sign of the pool getting deeper. However, there were some dark shadows about the size of half a basketball court that began to emerge into view beneath the water, indicating that there were big pits at the bottom of the pool. We did our best to avoid them and began to feel as though we were heading into trouble again.

Fats found another carved sign on a rock formation and we all stopped to examine it. It pointed us in a different direction from the one we'd been following. We carried on and soon found the third engraved mark on a pillar. Wen-Jin looked at Qilin, but before she could speak, he said, "This is the last one. We're almost there."

The last one—the last sign—our next stop would be our final destination. We set off in the direction the sign had given us and the back of my neck stiffened with tension.

Somehow I knew that we weren't heading toward a happy ending.

After a few steps beyond the sign, my right foot began to sting painfully. "I've stepped on something—watch out," I called to the others. "It feels like I walked on some broken glass. Fats, shine your flashlight over here, will you?"

My heel streamed blood from a large cut; something had sliced through my boot and sock into my bare flesh. I looked down to see what had caused it and saw objects that gleamed brightly in the water, like little pebbles with strange shapes. I bent down and picked one up; it was a piece of shattered porcelain, exactly like the pottery that we found in the desert shipwreck. But here, scattered on the bottom of the pool were thousands of fragments along with unbroken porcelain objects that were partially buried in the gravel, extending in every direction as far as our eyes could see.

CHAPTER TWENTY-THREE
THE GOAL

Fats leaned over to pick up a graceful jug that glittered with an azure glaze. "Oh shit," he yelped, "there are human skulls down here too." He held one up for us to see; its bones were rotting away but its hair was as luxuriant as the Forbidden Lady's, and I shuddered at her memory.

"These jars were farms for sacrifices," I explained, and told him what we had discovered earlier at the ship in the desert. "This place must be a religious site where the sacrificial offerings for the snakes were fed, cared for, and then killed. But I don't think these skulls hold corpse-eaters, after being in this frigid water for centuries. Those bugs would have frozen to death or drowned a thousand years ago."

"With all of these sacrificial vessels lying around, do you think the Queen of the West is buried down here?" Mop asked.

"Why speculate when we can find out for ourselves?" Fats replied. "Be careful where you step—these skulls could be poisonous. We may have to amputate Young Wu's foot before too long. And watch out for snakes while you're at it."

"Thanks for the reassurance, Fats. And speaking of

snakes, it's weird that we haven't come across any for such a long time. Where did those little monsters go anyway?" Even snakes were a better topic of discussion than whether or not my foot needed to come off. I hoped it was a shard of porcelain that had sliced into my foot and not one of those damned skulls.

We moved forward, being careful of where we placed our feet. The water became almost transparent, and there was more porcelain than I had ever seen in one place before. In less than a mile, we found ourselves on a shoal that was completely made up of bits of porcelain.

Big and small pieces covered the entire area, mostly dark red and yellow. Buried under the fragments were countless layers of unbroken jars of skulls. Thinking of how many human heads were at the bottom of the pool was beginning to nauseate all of us.

"Let's find another route," I gulped, trying not to vomit as I spoke, and the others nodded, looking green themselves. But we couldn't get out of the realm of skull jars.

Wen-Jin had been silent for hours so when her voice broke the stillness, we all stopped in our tracks. "Wait a minute," she said, "I think we're exactly where we want to be."

"You mean we've reached our goal?" I asked.

She nodded. "It looks like we've reached a place where there's an accumulation of sacrificial offerings, which usually means it's a sacred spot. I think this is the end right here."

I looked around and felt disappointed and depressed. We had gone through so much horror and death to end up in a pool full of skulls. What was the point? Where were the answers to the questions that had driven me here? It all seemed pointless—Ning's death, Panzi wounded beyond repair, the knowledge that my uncle wasn't who I'd always thought he was—and for what?

I looked at Qilin; he was inscrutable. Wen-Jin directed her flashlight into the pool and we all did the same thing. The only discovery we made was a large number of skull jars, layers and layers of them. Could what we were seeking lie below them? But who knew what we were looking for? Only Qilin—and he couldn't remember.

I drew back my injured foot and kicked the water in frustration and disappointment. Suddenly my reflection was clearly visible in the pool, distorted so my face looked as though it was pasted on my stomach. I looked at the water close by; nobody else was reflected in its depths.

Somewhere there was a light that was shining above only me. I beamed my flashlight up at the ceiling of the cave and yelped with a surprise that went beyond any words. Directly above me was an enormous sphere, so huge that it filled my entire field of vision. It looked as though it was made of stone, but not the same material that made up the rest of the cave. And strangest of all, it was covered with thousands of holes, each one the size of a 50-gallon barrel, looking as though it had been devoured by gargantuan worms.

Everyone else followed my gaze and stood frozen by the sight. Fats stammered his usual "What the hell…" and Wen-Jin murmured, "It's a stone from heaven. I never thought I would see one."

CHAPTER TWENTY-FOUR
THE STONE FROM HEAVEN

Since meteorites fall out of the sky, our ancestors had called them stones from heaven. We knew this had to be a meteorite, because no humans could have embedded such a colossal boulder within the ceiling of a cave. The part that we could see was probably 3,200 feet in diameter; it was impossible to imagine the size of the portion embedded in the rock.

The holes on the meteorite made it look vaguely disgusting, as though it were a giant, decaying honeycomb. They looked like a million tiny eyes that were watching us and they made me feel very uncomfortable. For some reason, I had a hunch that they were connected to the immortality pills we had found earlier.

Wen-Jin said, "This must be our destination. This has to be the ultimate secret of the Queen of the West. Wang Canghai was probably searching for this very thing."

"What the hell did he want this for?" I couldn't quite understand.

Wen-Jin shook her head. "I don't know. It might have something to do with the holes in the stone of heaven. Why are there so many of them?"

I felt my back turn to ice as I looked at those holes. "Could they have been artificially scooped out? Shit—could there be something inside this meteorite?"

The Sunglasses Kid suddenly said, "No. These are probably natural holes. Many meteorites look like honeycombs, but this one is hideous."

"Have you guys heard of an unconfirmed theory that the Qaidam Basin and the Tarim Basin were both formed by an asteroid that struck the earth? This thing might be one of the remaining meteorite fragments from that time," one of Uncle Three's men broke in. "The oasis of Tamu-Tuo was supposedly the eye of the asteroid crash. When the subjects of the Queen of the West were building her city right here at the center, while constructing the underground reservoir, they discovered this meteorite deep within the bowels of the earth. I think this might be the symbol of the Queen of the West's spiritual power."

This was the first time this guy ever talked. Just as I was about to ask him to explain his theory in detail, Fats captured my attention.

He and Qilin had wandered away from the rest of us and were examining a spot that I couldn't see from where I stood. Fats was waving his arms like a maniac and yelling, "Come over here!"

We all waded to his side, which was the spot where the meteorite and the cave's ceiling had collided. It was covered with stone pillars, dripping from the ceiling so close together that they looked like sculpted waterfalls. They were slanted at a gentle pitch, forming a ramp that we could easily climb to get a closer look at the meteorite.

As we made our ascent we saw a primitive set of steps

on the widest of the rock "waterfalls." On both sides of the stone steps stood many bronze lamps. At the top of the stairs was the conjunction of the rock waterfall and the ceiling of the cave, which was shaped by builders to form a stone platform. I looked around and realized this must be the sacrificial altar. The platform was as close to the meteorite as it could possibly be, while providing a panoramic view of the ritual sacrifice.

The most stunning sight was a huge throne built from the rock on the platform. I couldn't see it very clearly, but there was someone was sitting upon it.

My breath became stuck in my throat and my mind began to race in circles.

"Who is this? Could it be the Queen of the West? After all these centuries, could she still be presiding over her sacred place?" I thought I was muttering to myself, but my speculations were clearly audible.

"This can't be the Queen of the West," Fats argued. "She's dead and buried or lying preserved in a coffin. It's impossible that she'd be left sitting on her throne—what we're seeing has to be a statue."

"No, it isn't," Wen-Jin said with complete conviction. "We haven't seen one human figure carved in stone anywhere around here. Why would there be one in the holy shrine of the Queen of the West? This figure here is no small matter. We've got to be careful."

"It's beyond my rifle's range," Fats observed. "Too bad Panzi's gun was destroyed, or I could fire a shot from this distance and know whether it's human or a ghost."

"If it were a ghost, you wouldn't be able to kill it. If it were human, you'd become a murderer," I told him and for once, Fats shut up.

Nevertheless, we had to get past that spot if we wanted to get closer to the meteorite. We all stood close together as we approached the stone steps.

The steps were crudely constructed and uneven; it took all of our attention to climb them, as slowly as though our feet had been dipped in lead. Bronze lamp holders on either side of the stairs were so rusted that one crumbled to bits when Fats grabbed it. Slowly we approached the platform; beneath the rays of our flashlight we could see the person on the throne. It was the corpse of a woman.

She wore an ornate crown and her gown was spun gold studded lavishly with pieces of dark jade. Her body sat rigidly in place and looked as though she could stand at any moment. Her face was blue, but as we looked we realized it had been covered with a cerulean powder that covered every bit of visible skin. She looked like a statue from a temple, perfect in every detail.

Behind her stood two guards, clad in suits of armor. The powder on their faces wasn't as carefully applied as it was on the woman they guarded; it was cracked and flaking away, revealing their rotten bones underneath.

"Could this really be the Queen of the West?" Fats whispered.

I nodded. "Looks like it. I would have never thought she'd still be here. Her ancient nobles must have placed her here after her body was embalmed."

Fats caught sight of the pieces of jade and in a second his eyes shone with greed. "Finally something worthwhile for me. Who would have ever figured that this bitch would be so well dressed—couldn't let go of her wealth even after she died."

I grabbed him before he could move and Qilin spoke up immediately. "Don't get too close." He pointed to a pattern carved on the floor around the throne, an image of a human-faced bird with a small body and a big head. The pattern made a disc that encircled the queen's resting place. Touching the edge of the disc with his oddly long fingers, he said, "There's a small gap right here. This might be a trap. Don't go near her."

Looking up, we saw that the surface of the meteorite was almost right above the tops of our heads. We could touch it with our hands if we jumped. There were a few deep holes right above us. After shining our flashlights into them, we found that these bottomless tunnels seemed to go all the way to the interior of the meteorite. Moreover, the walls of these long tunnels were very smooth, indicating that they couldn't possibly have been excavated by men.

Why did Wang Canghai come here to look for this? If what Wen-Jin said was true, that he had come to discover the secret of achieving immortality, what did this meteorite have to do with that knowledge?

I looked up to study the meteorite more carefully, and as I looked I suddenly discovered something strange.

Why was this meteorite so similar to the jade statues we had seen in the cave with the astrolabe? The dark color and the sheen of the stone of heaven seemed identical to what had covered the bodies that had emerged as blood zombies. I jumped up to touch the surface of the meteorite and found that it was moist but not cold. It really felt and looked like jade.

24. THE STONE FROM HEAVEN

Holy shit, I thought. Could this be a jade meteorite?

There is a special kind of gem in the world called jade meteorite that in ancient times was very precious. Because the texture of its material is very similar to jade, people often confuse the two. However, the color of this meteorite was much darker than the ancient gemstone. Could this be a jade meteorite that contained some special properties? If this were true, then this discovery was valuable beyond comprehension. Each of us would become millionaires even if we sold it by the half ton.

I announced my thoughts and everyone was in full agreement.

"The gold-threaded jade burial shroud began gaining popularity in the Han dynasty. Legend has it that it could prevent corpses from rotting for a thousand years. But where did this legend come from in the first place? Could the alchemists who studied ancient texts have found descriptions of corpses preserved with jade burial shrouds without realizing the coverings were made from jade meteorite, not normal jade? What do you guys think?"

"Could this have been written in the silk book of the Warring States period?" Fats suggested. "Are you saying that the production of jade burial shrouds in the Han dynasty was a flawed imitation of the jade meteorite creations described in the silk books?"

"That's a possibility," I said, nodding. "And Wang Canghai discovered this mistake, so he began to search for the real material that was mentioned in the ancient books."

Everything seemed much clearer to me now. "If that's true, then all of the grave-robbing activities Wang

Canghai conducted were in search of this jade meteorite. And when he finally discovered its location, he took a team of men to come here with him."

"No." Wen-Jin wasn't nearly as excited as I was. "If it were really as you say, then he would have succeeded just by reaching this place. But we found no jade statues in the undersea tomb. This meteorite wasn't Wang Canghai's goal."

"Then what was his goal?" I asked.

Looking up at the holes in the meteorite, Wen-Jin said, "I don't know. But I have a feeling that the answer is inside these holes."

Her words were eerie and my mind went blank. I stared up at the holes, wondering what could be inside.

Wen-Jin took a rope out of her backpack. "I have to go and see for myself."

"No!" I shouted. I reached out to stop her but Qilin blocked my path. We stood eye to eye for a minute and then I understood. Wen-Jin had to do this and nothing I said or did would change her mind.

I stood aside, feeling powerless. Only when someone can offer no help will he feel so small. I always thought that this sadness only happened on television shows; I never thought I would feel this way.

Wen-Jin's preparations were swift and she soon was ready to move into the hole. As I watched, I realized she was the only one of us who was small enough to make this exploratory maneuver. And she was also in the best physical shape, after her life of evading snakes in the swampland.

Qilin knotted the rope around her waist and she climbed up on Fats's shoulders. With one leap, she was inside the opening. "Be careful!" I shouted. She looked at me with an expression I couldn't understand, then smiled and disappeared down the dark tunnel of the hole.

What could she be feeling right now, I wondered. I was always terrified when I crawled down a robber's tunnel, but that had the logic of a man-made passageway. This was without any rational construction; it was more like crawling down the throat of a whale. Who knew where she might end up? If anything happened to her, none of us would be able to get into the hole to rescue her.

The long rope that was attached to Wen-Jin's waist continued to slither into the tunnel. Every thirty feet or so, Fats would tug on it and a corresponding tug came back from the depths of the hole. "She's still alive," he muttered, each time his signal was returned. No other words were spoken. We all found it was hard to breathe.

After about an hour, Fats cursed quietly and I leaped to my feet.

"What's wrong?"

"She's not responding to my tugs now." He pulled on the rope and several feet slithered back to him, but nothing pulled it back up into the hole.

"Do it again," I yelled.

He did. A longer length returned to us and he frowned. "This isn't good. It feels loose, as though it isn't tied to her anymore."

Qilin turned ashen. "Pull her out of there right now!"

Fats quickly pulled at the rope; it came out in a clump, all of it to the very end, falling directly on me and wrapping around my body.

I grabbed the tail end and looked at it carefully; there were no rips in the strands nor signs of being cut. Wen-Jin had untied the knot herself. But why did she do it?

Qilin looked as I had never seen him before, as though his heart had just broken. Before we could stop him, he leaped up on Fats's shoulders and jumped into the tunnel, constricting his bones as only he could. "The rope! Take the damned rope!" Fats screamed but Qilin was gone.

"Bend down," I told Fats.

"No," he shouted. "I'm not here to be everybody's goddamned ladder. Forget it."

I pulled myself onto his back and squirmed onto his shoulders but I couldn't make the leap into the tunnel. I fell hard, directly back onto Fats, who grabbed me by the shoulders and shook me until I thought my nose would fall off. "You're not built to be a hero, you damned idiot. Stop this bullshit now."

I stood up and saw Qilin slowly crawling out of sight, and a weird thought struck me. Could this meteorite be alive? Were these holes and tunnels traps to catch food? Were Wen-Jin and Qilin delivering themselves into its snare?

They were both gone now. I sat and stared at the opening, hoping to see them safely return to us. For hours I waited, feeling worry turn to numbness and then going from numb into a complete blank. I felt nothing at all; there was too much to feel.

Ten hours later, there was still no sign or sound coming from the dark hole. It was as though Wen-Jin and Qilin had gone down this tunnel and entered another world.

We waited for three days. The only thing that I paid attention to was the tunnel opening into which they had disappeared. I tried more than once to enter it, but all my attempts had ended in failure. The farthest I managed to get was thirty feet in before the walls became so narrow I couldn't put my hand inside the space between them. I came back out with my trembling legs as useless as two cooked noodles. Not even the Sunglasses Kid made an effort to go into the hole after he saw what it had done to me.

"Let's get out of here," Mop urged us. "Those two are dead for sure and we will be too if we don't leave soon."

I refused to listen to him. Our journey couldn't end this way. All I could think of was what had happened and how I could possibly make sense of any of it.

Wen-Jin had deliberately untied the rope. I remembered the expression on her face just before she smiled at me; I had the feeling she had planned this long ago. This meant that she knew what she would encounter inside the meteor and that she was aware that she probably wouldn't make it back out alive. If it were true that her fate was to turn into a monster, she really had nothing to lose. But did Qilin feel that way too? I felt sure there was something they couldn't fight against that had taken them from us.

My thoughts began to drift. Could they have gotten lost? The meandering pathways within might have formed an endless maze, trapping them inside forever. But that didn't explain why Wen-Jin untied the rope.

Every single thought in my mind disturbed me;

whether I lay down to rest with my eyes open or closed, that deep tunnel was all I could see.

There was still no sign of life in the tunnel. Sometimes I even wondered if Wen-Jin and Qilin had ever existed or if they were merely figments of my imagination.

Then things went truly straight to hell. Mop and his group began to complain without stopping for breath. It was almost unbearable and I had to stop Fats from sending a few bullets their way. They finally left, with the Sunglasses Kid following them. He tried to persuade Fats and me to leave too, but we refused. Later we found they had taken most of our food when they left, but that didn't seem important to me at all.

"Are you sure you want to stay, Young Wu?" Fats asked me once. Then we both sat together in silence, staring at the tunnel and waiting.

Why had I come to this place? Could everything end right here? I remembered a theater of the absurd drama called *Waiting for Godot*, and my throat tightened at the memory. Our own absurd drama has become a tragedy, I thought, trying to make a private joke and failing badly. Although I didn't realize it, I was close to madness, so depressed I couldn't think at all.

One night I woke up to the sound of Fats snoring. I walked over to the bottom of the tunnel opening and looked up at it. There was nothing and nobody there. Realizing I hadn't eaten for a day or two, I went to our small supply of food and began to gnaw at a biscuit. As I chewed, a strange sound floated through the air, sounding partly like someone singing and partly like the groans people make while they're sleeping.

24. THE STONE FROM HEAVEN

I thought Fats was talking in his sleep so I didn't pay any attention. When I finished eating, I walked over to wake him up. Someone else was lying nearby; it was Qilin, wrapped in a blanket, gaunt, pale, and motionless.

When did he come back? Was it when I was still asleep?

At first I thought I was dreaming, but when I found out I wasn't, I nearly went insane. I rushed over to him, pulled away his blanket, and screamed, "You bastard! Where the fuck did you go?"

I gripped him tightly, wanting nothing more than to punch him in the face, but there was something terribly wrong with him. His expression was strange, his eyes were wide open but vacant, and his whole body was trembling. His lips quivered without stopping, as if he was trying to speak.

My heart turned cold and I gave Fats a quick push to wake him up. Then I propped Qilin into a sitting position and called out his name. He didn't seem to hear me. He didn't respond or react or even blink.

A rush of terror surged through me. Fats came over, looked at us, and asked me what was going on. I told him what I knew, and he pressed Poker-face's temples with his thumbs. "He has no reflexes at all. What could have happened to him? Has he gone insane?"

"That's impossible. Stop talking nonsense," I said. I leaned toward Qilin, shouting as loud as I could, "Stop pretending! I know you're just pretending. You can't fool me!"

Still trembling, Qilin backed into a corner, staring at me with white eyes and mouthing something over and over.

24. THE STONE FROM HEAVEN

"I can't hear you. Speak up." I sat closer to him and realized he was repeating one sentence, rapidly and in a hollow tone of voice.

"There is no time," he muttered; then he shut his eyes and fell into a deep sleep.

I watched him, feeling depressed and frightened. What had happened to put him in such a state? And what had become of Wen-Jin?

I looked up at the meteorite; now more than ever its many holes looked like eyes, following every move we made, plotting our deaths.

"There is no time." What did that mean? It sounded as though something horrible was going to happen soon, and there was nothing we could do about it.

Fats sat down beside me and sighed heavily. "He must have been struck by something really unexpected. He can't hear, he can't see; all his senses are shut down. It's as though he's been buried alive. One of my friends is catatonic like that; his doctor said his brain was paralyzed within the moment of his last experience."

I didn't say a word. I knew that it would be almost impossible for Qilin to be shocked by things that would annihilate anybody else. Whatever happened to him inside this meteorite must have been more terrifying than anything Fats or I could imagine. What could be so frightening that it would cause Qilin to break down as he had? Was it something that had hurt Wen-Jin? Had she gone mad and was she trapped within the meteorite? If that were true, I had to get in there somehow and save her.

Once again I stood up, walked to the tunnel opening, turned on the flashlight, and pointed it upward. I had done this so many times that it had almost become automatic. But this time something was different—the tunnel was no longer pitch-black. Something shone through the darkness.

"Fats, get over here," I shouted as I turned up the beam of my flashlight and shone it into the tunnel. A pale face peered back at me and I cried out, "Wen-Jin, is that you?"

But then I took a second look and began to tremble. The fish-belly-white, expressionless face with eyes sunk deep in its sockets was one I'd never seen before.

Fats saw it too and rushed off to get his rifle but as he moved, the face disappeared and the tunnel was black once more.

This matter had gone beyond my scope of understanding. How could there be someone inside this meteorite? Could there be people living in it? Could descendants of the Queen of the West still dwell in this dark and gigantic rock?

Then I thought of Wen-Jin again and my heart almost stopped. Could she have started going through the horrible change she had told me about? Was this her face?

I looked at Fats, wanting to ask him if he could pinpoint any feature on this face that looked like Wen-Jin, but he was staring into the tunnel, pale and terrified. He turned back and asked me, "You didn't recognize her?"

"Recognize her?" I froze for a moment before continuing, "You know this person?"

Fats gestured behind us. I turned around and saw the corpse of the woman sitting on the throne. Fats pointed the miner's lamp to the face of the corpse. The light flashed, producing an effect of light and shadow that made the woman's face seem strikingly hideous.

I understood what he meant at once. My realization sent chills down my spine and I almost fainted. The face we were looking at now looked almost exactly the same as the face in the tunnel.

"What's going on? Could the face that we just saw be— the Queen of the West? Could this corpse be a shell? Is the real Queen of the West still alive in the center of this damned rock?" Fats asked.

"Impossible. How could that be? How could someone who existed thousands of years ago still be alive? Even if she hadn't died of old age, she would have starved to death centuries ago. At this point, how can we trust our own senses, after all that we've gone through? That face just now might have been Wen-Jin's, with the dark shadows making her appear like this enthroned corpse."

Fats frowned. "Then why didn't she come out?"

"Young Wu," he continued after a slight pause, "this place is getting worse and worse by the minute. When do you plan to leave?"

"What? Wen-Jin hasn't come back out yet." I couldn't shake away the look on his face and asked, "Why are you so scared? It's not like you."

"We don't have much left to eat. I was going to talk to you today. If you refused to leave tomorrow, I was planning to just knock you out and take you with me. If we keep waiting, we'll starve to death."

"Can't we hold out for a few more days?"

Fats said, "I've done the calculations. We have enough for two more days if we watch our portions, which is just enough time to get us back to the real world—but that isn't taking Qilin into consideration. Now it's even more critical. If we don't leave immediately, we'll all die here."

I looked up at the tunnel and shook my head. "No. I'm not leaving Wen-Jin."

Fats grabbed my arm. "What good will we be to her, if she comes out to find us all dead? And don't forget about Qilin—even if you're willing to die, he might not feel the same way. At least we'll be able to save one of them. And we'll leave some food in case Wen-Jin emerges."

"All right, Fats. You win. We'll leave—but which way should we go?"

"We'll backtrack. Then we'll walk along the river wall. The other water outlet should be somewhere over there. From there we'll get back to the reservoir again, and there we'll certainly find an exit."

"And if we can't?"

"We can't think about that now. We can only let fate take its course. But I think there's an exit, or the Sunglasses Kid would've come back a long time ago."

Fats began to pack up our equipment and we soon set off, supporting Qilin's unconscious form between us. Soon we returned to the stream with the broken and buried porcelain and Fats stopped. In front of us was a deep pit that hadn't been there before.

"There's something wrong here—don't stop, Fats."

"Look—can't you see a light flashing at the bottom of this pit? There might be something good down there. I'm going to go down and take a look. Wait for me. I'll be back in a few minutes."

There was nothing I could do to stop him so I stood, holding Qilin on my own while Fats followed his greed. He soon returned with blood pouring from a deep cut on his hand, clutching something that looked like a bone.

"What is that?" I asked.

"Damned if I know, but it feels as though it's hiding thorns somewhere. Shine your flashlight over so I can take a closer look."

"Serves you right." I muttered as I walked over with my flashlight. Just as I got to his side, a series of rumbling sounds came from below my feet, followed by a string of water bubbles erupting to the water surface.

Fats and I both froze. The water bubbles paused, and then the rumbling gushed up once again.

"God damn it. I have to salute you—you fart like a rocket launcher." Fats covered his nose.

"Fats, that wasn't me."

"If you didn't fart, then why does it stink? What kind of smell is this? It could be used as a lethal weapon." Fats frowned.

The air was filled with a horrible stench and I knew we had to leave fast. Before I could speak, I lost my footing, the water surface exploded with a series of splashes, and I sank deep into nothingness as though the ground had disappeared below me.

I tried to regain my footing but there was only water, so I dove beneath it, with Fats following my example. Where Qilin might be, I had no idea.

As Fats and I swam, we saw the pit below us had become much larger with the collapse of the streambed. Porcelain and bones were careening toward the edge of the abyss, and Qilin was being swept along with the debris. His legs were buried in the mass of objects and he was passively allowing himself to be carried to his death.

Fats and I rushed to his side, grabbed him by the arms, and pulled him free. He began to cough as soon as we all got above the surface of the water, with firm footing beneath us.

The stench was worse than ever and bubbles continued to issue from the pit. "I know what this stink is," I announced. "It's marsh gas and it's pushing its way to the surface. That's what caused this pit to open up and that's what's making it increasingly larger."

"You may be right," Fats admitted, "but what the hell is that?" He jerked his chin in the direction of his flashlight.

Something was floating up from the middle of the pit. Fats reached out and grabbed at it. It was a clump of rotting tree branches with cotton wrapped around it.

"It's nothing important—let's get the hell out of here, Fats," I pleaded.

We covered our noses, and just as we were about to set off, Fats picked up something else as it floated by. He raised it high in the air and gasped, "Holy shit. Look at this."

CHAPTER TWENTY-FIVE

A CANTEEN

I looked toward him and thought I saw a small head without a face, covered with black mud and small tentacles.

"What the hell is it?" I asked.

Fats threw it over and I caught it in midair. Rinsing it in the stream, I found a green, rusty surface under the mud. "Damn, it's a military canteen, an old one made a few decades ago. I can tell by its shape. I've got one just like it at home. What's going on? Why would there be a canteen floating up from this pit?"

"Could it belong to the armed revolutionaries that fled here twenty years ago or so?"

"Maybe," I replied. "But that's not the problem. The question is how this thing got down there."

"Maybe a revolutionary came here and just happened to have been killed in this hole."

Before I could reply, I suddenly felt a twitching motion below the soles of my feet. I threw out my arms to keep my balance and yelled, "Watch out—we're in for another collapse."

I looked down at the pit and saw a huge flash of scales floating up toward us and a pair of yellow eyes the size of two basketballs. I stared in shock, frozen in place.

Fats saw it too and pushed me, shouting, "Run, damn you!" He began to drag me along with him. I grabbed Qilin's arm and raced away as fast as I could.

But it was impossible to be swift with the water resistance working against us and the sharp fragments of porcelain beneath our feet. Something jabbed my foot and I fell, with Qilin and Fats plunging down beside me. Fats was the first to scramble back on his feet and pulled both of us up with him. "Don't stop," he shouted.

There was a deafening sound of splashing water; I looked back and saw a mammoth reptile shooting up from the water like a mythical dragon. This had to be the basilisk, the serpent mother-goddess that the other reptiles cared for and kept alive, the snake we had seen depicted in the wall carvings.

"We're finished!" I groaned, but I gritted my teeth and continued to run. Water splashed behind me like monstrous waves but after that one glance, I refused to look back. Adrenaline took over; I ran, fell, got back up, and continued with no thought of anything but my own survival. As I mindlessly raced along the streambed, I tripped and plunged into a pit. Fats saw me go under and ran back to save me, but before I could grasp his hand, there was a flash of scales. A wave of force swept over the surface of the water, knocking both Fats and Qilin down to my level.

The huge reptile curled around the area we were in. Fats pulled out his knife, but compared to the size of this monster, it was no more than a toothpick. The basilisk dove toward us, its head inches away and its scales blinding us like a thousand mirrors in the sun. It is really a water dragon, I thought, stupefied by what I saw; this is what grabbed and disposed of the owner of the canteen. Now it's our turn.

We struggled in the water, trying to swim out of the corral made by the python's body, but we found it was impossible to control our body movements. When the serpent moved, the water current pushed us down and changed the direction of our motion.

"We're dead, Fats. We can't win against this monster," I said.

"No," he shouted. "Elephants don't eat ants. We're too small for this serpent. It won't be so easy for it to gobble us down."

As if it heard his challenge, the basilisk drew back its head and opened its mouth as it swam toward Fats. Its momentum was like the force of a hurricane, and I was instantly tossed some distance away by the churning of the waves.

I came up to the surface, shouting for Fats, and was surprised to see that the serpent had missed him. He was still holding onto Qilin and they were both a short distance from where I was.

Having missed its target, the python was out for blood. It coiled its body to form a huge wave and its glittering scales formed a wall of mirrors that was terrible to look at.

"Hide!" Fats's shout echoed through the water and I swam to the back of a rock outcropping, climbing to its top. Waiting for me there was the head of the snake, staring at me with its basketball eyes. I was too terrified to breathe, let alone think. This was it.

Seconds passed with no attack. What was keeping this thing from finishing me off? I had nothing but my flashlight, which mercifully was waterproof. Then I realized this monster had been underwater for years and my light had it at a loss. If I put the flashlight on this outcropping, I might be able to escape while the basilisk was hypnotized by its beam.

Yet there was no level spot where I could put the flashlight. Once I let go of it, it would slip down into the stream. There had to be another way out—I just had to think clearly.

Suddenly I saw Fats behind the snake's head, gesturing to me to throw the flashlight over to him.

I took a deep breath and tossed the flashlight into the air. It sailed toward Fats in an arc of light and the basilisk's gaze followed it. When its eyes left me, I dove into the water.

The snake plunged after me but I swam for my life, not coming to the surface until I was exhausted. I could see that I hadn't gone very far. The basilisk was right behind me—and then it was gone.

Soon I saw Fats with Qilin on his back, wading quickly in my direction.

"What happened? What did you do to that thing?" I asked.

"I tossed your flashlight down into the pit. The serpent's gone to retrieve it. We have to get out of here because as soon as it comes back up, we'll be dead."

We ran, gasping for air, not daring to stop for a second. We reached the reservoir channel, randomly chose a direction, and walked along the wall in search of an exit, exhausted and starving.

"We can go for a week or two without eating, just by burning the fat on our bodies. The worst part will be the first few days," Fats said. "I've gone through this before—we'll be okay."

Qilin remained in his trance; slowly he got better but he remembered nothing at all.

We talked to him about everything that had happened, but he couldn't make sense of any of it. The only good thing was we didn't have to carry him anymore.

We began to catch insects for food, which kept us going. Finally we saw some living tree roots clinging to the tunnel walls and Fats announced that we were close to an exit. Sure enough we found a shaft leading upward. Fats climbed through it and found that this was where the towers with square windows were, the ones we had passed earlier at the beginning of this debacle. We squeezed our way through and were back in the world at last.

Everything had changed dramatically. The water level of the swamp had gone down to almost nothing, exposing the mud and the savage-looking root systems. All of the trees were covered with blossoms. The sun shone hot and bright, driving all the snakes into the dark cool refuge underground. We were safe for now.

The brilliance of the sun, the songs of the birds, and the fragrance of the flowers painted an idyllic scene in this jungle that could easily fool a man into believing it was a paradise on earth. But we knew that was only an illusion. There was no time to rest, no matter how peaceful this place appeared.

"We'll get to the canyon, but we won't make it out of there before dark," Fats said, "the farthest we'll get will be somewhere in its center. And if we come across any problems, we're so weak that we won't survive. From here on out, it's all a matter of luck."

I tried not to think of Panzi or the man I had called Uncle Three—or Wen-Jin. Even if we survived, their memories would keep my life from ever being the same.

We spent a day and a night crossing the canyon. When we got back to the desert, we found Dingzhu-Zhuoma waiting for us. Fats almost fainted when he saw her, and I felt as though I had been reborn. When we walked toward the old lady she rushed toward us and pinched us hard to be certain that we weren't ghosts.

We rested in the camp for three days, exhausted, vacant, and listless. I didn't think about anything during that time; I didn't even feel sad or depressed. All I knew was that sleep was the most important thing—nothing else mattered. For the first time, I felt relieved, as though the mysteries and unsolved questions of this adventure had nothing to do with me at all.

Qilin showed no improvement. He either huddled in a corner of his tent in a daze, or sprawled against a rock, staring at the sky. Fats and I felt bad for him, but there was nothing we could do. Who would have thought that he would pursue this quest all the way to the end only to lose himself?

The miracle was that Panzi was still alive. Tashi had found him while looking for us. He was now lying in another tent, sometimes conscious and sometimes locked in a coma. I didn't dare tell him the things I'd learned about his Master Three.

We rested for two more days and then Tashi said we should make our way back. According to what he had been told, we were now in the middle of a long chain of ghost cities. Meticulous traps had been set in these cities so we had to navigate with extreme caution and accuracy. Once we got out, there would be highways running both east and west. When we were safely on one of them, we'd be able to seek help.

I was haunted by the question of whether the Sunglasses Kid and the man who used to be my uncle had survived somehow, but Tashi was realistic about their chances. "Either they've come out from another entrance, or they haven't come out at all. But there's nothing we can do about that now." He shrugged, and of course he was right.

We had no vehicles so we walked. We carried nothing but water.

"We can live without food, or even tents, but not without water," Fats said. "We need to use all of our strength to carry as much water as possible." We followed his advice and, laden with canteens, we began to cross the Gobi Desert. Four days later we were out of the chain of ghost cities and after another week, we hit a highway. A military transport let us use their phone and thirty hours later, a fleet of cars from Ning's company showed up to rescue us.

On the way back, Fats leaned against the backseat of the car and began to sing.

The gonglike music of his voice was quite pleasant, and I suddenly felt a burst of melancholy. I burst into tears, my vision blurred, the past flashed across my eyes like a nightmare, and I could hear the voices of those who were forever lost to me, echoing in the vast Gobi Desert.

After we were safely in Golmud, I weighed the pros and cons repeatedly before sitting down to write an e-mail to Uncle Two, telling him everything that happened. In half an hour, he called me, telling me that I mustn't talk about this to anyone else. "Don't worry anymore. I'll deal with this matter from now on. Now, please, Nephew," he concluded, "hurry home to Hangzhou."

Obviously I couldn't go back immediately. Qilin, Panzi, and Fats all needed to be hospitalized. Fats was suffering from overexertion; after getting a few bottles of liquid nutrients pumped into his bloodstream through an IV, he slowly got better. Panzi, to everyone's amazement, survived. When I told him about Uncle Three, he was overwhelmed with disbelief and sorrow. He left the hospital against the doctor's orders and went home to Changsha, saying he would stay there until he had news about Master Three. Qilin was in the worst shape. He was unable to remember anything at all about any part of his past; he was confused by the smallest details of daily living and his doctors said he would need to rest quietly if he were ever to be his old self again.

When I visited him, he had no idea of who I was, which made me feel like falling apart. It was tougher and tougher to watch him as the days went by.

Finally I went home. There was a pile of mail waiting for me and as I went through it, I found a letter sent to me by Uncle Three.

I checked the date, but there was no postmark. I tore it open and found a long letter.

Nephew:

By the time you read this, I may be missing, or perhaps I will be dead.

I don't know if you know the truth by now, but no matter what, I owe you an explanation.

I'm about to do one thing right now. This is my fate; I can't escape it. I have a hunch that this might be the last thing I ever do. I've ruined my entire life for this, and if I can't find the answer, I would rather die.

I've written everything that you wanted to know below. You can take your time to read it. You have probably been very curious about why I lied to you again and again, but you'll understand after you finish reading. It's because I myself am a lie.

I am very sorry. But no matter what you think of me, to me, you'll always be my nephew. You have to believe me when I say that everything that I did, I did to protect you. I have never meant to harm you or any of the Wu family.

Perhaps I have actually become Wu Sansheng. Maybe I have been wearing this mask for so long, I can't take it off now.

And I'm sorry that I cannot explain everything in detail in this letter. But I do want to say that there are unavoidable reasons for everything that happened. I myself am merely a glitch in the story. A strange combination of circumstances led to these events, and once I was up to my neck in this whole thing, I could no longer redeem myself.

In fact, a much bigger secret is hidden behind the things that happened in Xisha. The backgrounds of Wen-Jin and the others aren't that simple either. When I was conducting an investigation on that entire team, I found out that several of them have no records at all. I have no idea where they came from and what they did in the past. If you investigate a little bit more, you'll find that this expedition is hiding something, and everything is very unpredictable. So if you choose to remain embroiled in this matter, you must turn to take a look at my fate. Then you'll know the price you will need to pay by searching for the truth behind this secret.

I hope that this will be the end of this whole matter for you, that after you learn the truth, you'll continue to live a full life instead of falling back into this same unsolvable snare. I know that you'll still find a lot of puzzles when you think of the whole thing, but none of this will have anything to do with you anymore.

As my final goodbye, I ask you to remember the words of

your grandfather:

What's even more frightening than ghosts is the will of men.

Your Uncle Three in Dunhuang

What he wrote next was exactly the same story that I had heard from Wen-Jin. As I read it, I was able to see fewer and fewer of the words on the page because my eyes were streaming with tears.

Three months after I came home from Golmud, I was still unable to shake off the nightmares that struck me—the same dreams every night made me relive everything that had happened. How could I get rid of them?

The secrets that had been unlocked didn't answer all of the questions that plagued me.

What others try desperately to cover up is inevitably something you don't want to see. So when searching for the truth behind other people's secrets, you have to accept the consequences that come with revealing what has been hidden. This was the lesson that I'd finally and painfully learned. But the price I paid was far less than the one Qilin faced every day, or Ning, or Wen-Jin—and that was hard for me to live with.

After my return, I wrote down everything that had happened on this strange quest, starting with my grandfather's journal all the way up to now. Everything, all of its details and even the parts that I wasn't certain about before, gradually became clear in my mind. The truth was always here; it was simple and obvious. Recalling how eager I had been to know the answers to these puzzles and how absurdly obsessed I had become filled me with a muddle of emotions once again.

When I finished writing my final words about our

adventures, I wondered when I would forget all these things. Right now it didn't seem possible that I ever would, but I knew that I'd forget one day, given enough time. I just wished that day would come sooner, rather than later.

There were so many things I still didn't know. Where was my real Uncle Three? Was was he dead or alive? Who was Qilin really? Where did Wen-Jin go? Who or what is *It*? What were the backgrounds of Wen-Jin and the students who went with her to Xisha and what kind of a plan were they carrying out? Who was the person who looked exactly like me who crawled like a madman on the floor of the old house in Golmud?

These things remained mysteries. In the beginning, I was obsessively concerned about them but now those questions didn't seem so important anymore—or so I told myself.

After Qilin left the hospital in Golmud, Fats and I sent him to the First Hospital at Beijing University for a thorough examination. His physical condition was almost perfect, but he still wasn't close to being mentally normal, so we left him at the hospital under the care of specialists. Meanwhile I asked around in Changsha, hoping to find out something about Qilin's background. I hired people to help me investigate but they were no more successful than I. It was much harder than I thought to uncover any information; he simply had to get better and perhaps he'd remember everything. If he didn't, then we'd just have to support him for the rest of his life.

Panzi had returned home to Changsha, where he found that the grave-robbing community was in absolute chaos without Master Three. He said he was ready to retire, after almost dying twice in the past year. "Find a girl and get married," I told him, and he replied, "Follow your own advice first, Young Master Wu. I'm busy enough just looking for Master Three and I won't rest until I find out whether he's alive or dead."

Fats was back in Beijing, immersed in his business ventures. Tashi had left us in Golmud, refusing to take any payment for bringing us safely out of the desert. Ning, of course, was dead. I tried to contact the company she'd worked for, hoping that the knowledge of her death would make Jude Kao give up this senseless enterprise that had brought so much grief to so many people.

Ashes to ashes, dust to dust, I told myself. Everyone's lives seemed to be returning to their normal paths. I settled back into my usual daily routine, selling old books and antiques, while feeling as though I'd time-traveled for a very long time, cut off from the world I'd once known.

When the legendary Zhuangzi had a dream about a butterfly, he awoke to find that he no longer knew if he was a man who had dreamed he was a butterfly, or a butterfly that was dreaming he was a man. I was always baffled when I'd heard the story in the past, but now I knew exactly how he felt. Which was real, my life now or the one I had as a grave robber? Each was its own separate realm of existence.

I often felt as though I were still in the middle of the graveyard of the queen, surrounded by snakes and swampland. I told myself this quest was finished and that I no longer cared about any of it, but truthfully I knew in the deepest core of my being that what had begun long ago with my grandfather in the cavern of the blood zombies was not yet at an end.

Note from the Author

Back in the days when there was no television or internet and I was still a poor kid, telling stories to other children was my greatest pleasure. My friends thought my stories were a lot of fun, and I decided that someday I would become the best of storytellers.

I wrote a lot of stories trying to make that dream come true, but most of them I put away, unfinished. I completely gave up my dream of being a writer, and like many people, I sat waiting for destiny to tap me on the shoulder.

Although I gave up my dream of being a writer, luckily the dream did not give up on me. When I was 26 years old, my uncle, a merchant who sold Chinese antiques, gave me his journal that was full of short notes he had written over the years. Although fragmentary information can often be quite boring, my uncle's writing inspired me to go back to my abandoned dream. A book about a family of grave robbers began to take shape, a suspenseful novel.... I started to write again....

This is my first story, my first book that became successful beyond all expectations, a best-seller that made me rich. I have no idea how this happened, nor does anybody else; this is probably the biggest mystery of The Grave Robbers' Chronicles. Perhaps as you read the many volumes of this chronicle, you will find out why it has become so popular. I hope you enjoy the adventures you'll encounter with Uncle Three, his nephew and their companions as they roam through a world of zombies, vampires, and corpse-eaters.

Thanks to Albert Wen, Michelle Wong, Janet Brown, Kathy Mok and all my friends who helped publish the English edition of The Grave Robbers' Chronicles.

Xu Lei was born in 1982 and graduated from Renmin University of China in 2004. He has held numerous jobs, working as a graphic designer, a computer programmer, and a supplier to the U.S. gaming industry. He is now the owner of an international trading company and lives in Hangzhou, China with his wife and son. Writing isn't his day job, but it is where his heart lies.